Tilted

Tilted

Nancy Hall

Library of Congress Cataloging-in-Publication Data

ISBN: 978-1-7333626-0-3

Printed and bound in the United States of America by
Ingram Lightning Source

First edition

Cover design: Wanda Stanfill

Editing, layout, and design: Jacque Hillman and Katie Gould

The HillHelen Group LLC
127 Fairmont Ave.
Jackson, TN 38301
hillhelengroup@gmail.com

For Dr. Stephen Mooney—
"Write something to change
their hearts, nothing less."

Acknowledgments

With a grateful heart, I wish to thank everyone for their support and especially:

My family, Jimmy, Greg, and Doug.

My parents, Bill and Johnye Fortner.

My friends, who encouraged me in ways you may never know.

My book club.

Jeannine Ouellette, my writing guru.

The inspiring experience and the women at the 2014 Elephant Rock Writing Retreat.

Victoria Matsui, Berlynne Holman, Donna Grear Parker, and Evelyn Lowery.

Wanda Stanfill, for the beautiful cover.

Jacque and Jesse Hillman and the staff at The HillHelen Group. This book would not have happened without you.

Most of all to my college teacher and dear friend Mooney, who taught me how to NOT write good girl prose. I wish you were here to see the results.

Contents

PART I
SPRING EQUINOX
MARCH 20, 1960

The Reason

When I decided to murder George, it was near the spring equinox, which was perfect; equinox means equal. It was time to set things right.

I looked at the farmers' almanac calendar hanging on my bedroom wall every morning. Each day stated the exact time of the sunrise, sunset, and moonrise. The position of the moon and the sign for the day were pictured there. I circled the official arrival of each season in red. Like a prisoner counting the days, I X'd off the seasons of my puny life.

The full moon had occurred on March 13 and was waning until March 21. I knew the waning moon was the time to correct mistakes, settle disputes, and make amends. The signs were right to act.

I had planned this for a very long time, and my gut told me to go ahead. Plus, I didn't like the way George was acting around Irene. I could not allow that. My kid sister with her blond hair and soft voice was not like me. She seemed to exist in another world. She was not as practical as me. She was content with old, faded dresses and shoes that were too big. We stuffed the toes of her hand-me-down shoes with newspaper. The kids at school teased her, but she hung her head and went on. Mother slapped her once at the supper table when she wouldn't eat. I can still see the shock in Irene's eyes and the red fingerprints on her cheek. She laid her head on the table, and the flies walked over her and into the cold food. I sneaked in later and threw the food out the back door and put her to bed.

Even though Irene was fourteen, she looked like she was ten. I hoped she had a bit of me in her, too, so she could make it. But I knew I couldn't leave her alone with George. I just couldn't. Besides, all of this was really his fault. He shouldn't have done what he did to me.

I planned to lure George out to the big gully on the back side of Mr. Perrigin's hog farm. The gully formed a natural barrier to insulate the shots, and it was about a quarter of a mile from Hale's Swamp. Nobody would be within hearing distance, especially this time of year. The red clay of the gullies used to be a perfect place to make hideouts when we were kids playing cowboys and Indians. It seemed like a good place for a shootout. Of course, only one of us would be doing the shooting. I had been preparing for this for about three years, but now I was scared and sick to my stomach. Something in my head just kept saying, "Do it, Meshac."

George was my mother's boyfriend. She brought him home after one of her nights of drinking when I was ten, and he stayed. That was seven years ago. He was a wiry little man about my height now and not much meat on his bones—just meanness. His knuckles were always skinned like he had been hitting something, and he smelled like coal oil. George went to town every Saturday afternoon to play cards at The Lounge and start his weekend drinking.

I was off work this Saturday and asked George if I could ride to town. I hadn't asked to be alone with him in that car ever. He looked at me kind of funny-like. I told him Katy was supposed to pick me up, but her daddy wouldn't let her have the car. "Fine," he said.

I already had my bag packed and told Mama I was staying over at Katy's for a couple of nights since I had to work at the cafe on Sunday before I went in at the sawmill on Monday. She never looked up at me. That's how I remember her, with her head down staring at the sunlight on the floor. Irene was already in town with our cousin, so that left my little brother Roy. I patted him on the head and squeezed his shoulder. He looked at me, and that was the last time I saw those brown eyes.

If things worked out, I would send money to Aunt Flora to help the kids. My backpack had a wad of money, about $500, and three of everything—underwear, pairs of socks, shirts, and jeans. I tucked in my favorite books—*O Pioneers!* and *Celestial Guide for Living by the Signs*. My black transistor radio and an old picture of Daddy and Mama and us kids lay on top. I only had one pair of shoes, and they were on my feet. I had already hidden my bedroll, canteen, flashlight, and the gun at the gully.

I got into the car with George. I could smell him, and I rolled down the window quickly. His hand reached up to shift gears, and for a moment I remembered his dirty, greasy hand closing around my neck. I didn't turn around and look at the house with its bare yard, stack of rotting wood, and Roy's wheel-less wagon. I held onto the door handle with my sweaty hands and tried to appear calm. George looked like he might be suspicious of something, but he didn't know just what. I tried to think of something to say but decided instead to say nothing.

Before we got to the turn in the road where the gullies started, I said casual-like, "I used to play down in those gullies when the kids and me were little."

George grunted.

"We used to think there was buried treasure down there." I looked straight ahead. "I wonder if those paw-paw bushes are still there. Do you like paw-paws, George?"

He waited a minute, then said, "Yeah, I used to eat 'em when I was a kid. My mama made some kind of jelly, I think."

"I want to see if they're still there."

George rolled his eyes. "It's too early."

"I know, but I want to see if the bushes are still there. You can stay here. I'll run down there."

His foot never let up, and I thought I had missed this chance.

"What the hell—okay," and he pulled over.

"It won't take me five minutes, I promise."

He turned into the field road that led into the pasture on the front of the property.

"How far is it?"

"About a hundred yards or so over that a way." I eased open the door, and as I got out, I said, "Be back in a jiffy."

I started down the field road in a trot. I needed to get a little lead on him. I started counting to myself—one Mississippi, two Mississippi. As soon as I went over the little rise, I took off running. I sprinted around the side of the field to the little copse of woods that hung on the edge of the gullies. The big gully backed up to one side like an amphitheater. My heart was pounding so hard my head hurt, and I couldn't catch my breath. I stopped when I was in the trees and looked back. No sign of him.

I climbed down the little hill to the hollow tree stump and dug out the tow sack. My hands shook so hard I couldn't unknot the drawstring. I felt the wet ground soaking my knees as I finally got the sack opened and pulled out the flannel-wrapped gun. I opened the chamber to be sure it was still loaded. Then I snapped it back together and held it with both hands as I stood up and kicked the sack behind the stump. I walked criss-cross back up the hill so I would emerge at the edge of the woods where the undergrowth was cleared out. All you could see was the red clay wall rising over the gully that plunged thirty feet down. There was a cedar tree there, and it tickled my neck as I leaned into it, waiting and hoping that George would come after me soon.

"You nasty old bastard, come on," I grumbled. "Don't let me lose my nerve."

About then I heard him holler. I waited for him to holler again, and then I shouted back, "Just a second." I saw him as he came up the rise. He looked mad, which made it even easier.

"Meshac, come on now, I gotta get to town."

I didn't say a word. "Come a little closer, you son of a bitch." It helped to whisper the words so I could hear them. Holding the gun with one hand, I wiped my sweaty hands, one at a time as fast as I could, on the back of my britches. He stopped and looked around. I sighted him down the barrel. I needed him to come a few yards closer. He looked around like a dang fox when the henhouse is empty.

"Meshac!" he bellowed.

I crouched back farther into the cedar tree and counted to five. "Over here," I shouted back.

He started walking toward me like a man on a mission. He must've seen some movement or the glint of the gun barrel. I tried to make myself wait one, two, three more steps, and then he looked right at me. It was still too far away. My legs were shaking, but I stepped out from the tree with the gun held straight in front of me.

"What are you doing?" Nastiness dripped out of his mouth.

"I'm fixing to kill you, George." I took two steps forward.

"What the hell you got?"

"I've got my daddy's gun, and I'm going to kill your ass dead."

He started to smile but then got this scared look like a mewling puppy.

"Give me that gun. You ain't gonna shoot nobody, you little whore."

As soon as he said that word, I felt my chest turn hot like a poker stabbing the middle of my heart. I didn't even take a deep breath. I walked a few steps closer; I didn't want to miss the son of a bitch. He picked up a big stick lying on the ground and started after me. "You ain't nothing but a little whore, and so's your sister."

He raised the stick over his head and took two more steps. I pulled the trigger two or three times. He looked shocked. I stood there and hoped he was going to die. He doubled over and stumbled a step or two and then fell face down on the ground. I'd like to say I felt bad afterward or I threw up or something, but I didn't. I broke out in a cold sweat, and my head got dizzy, but I rested my hands on my knees and hung my head until the dizziness went away. I could feel my eyes tear up, but I never stopped to wipe my face.

I don't know how long I stood to make sure he wasn't going to move. When I walked over to him, I didn't think I could see him breathing, but I wanted to be certain. I poked him with the toe of my muddy shoe. He didn't make a sound. I poked him again higher on his shoulder, and he lay there. I knew in that moment my life had changed forever. Even though

I was only seventeen years old, I had enough sense to know that nothing would ever be the same. But I had no regret in my heart—none at all.

He had started it one night when Mama was passed out. I slept in a double bed at the back of the house with Irene. She slept next to the wall. Something woke me up, and I could feel him there in the room. He touched my shoulder. I squinted my eyes tighter, trying to act like I was asleep. I could smell his breath before his words reached me.

"Meshac, get up. Now."

He grabbed my arm and lifted me out of the bed onto my bare feet. I felt like I was going to wet myself right then.

"What is it, George?"

"Come out to the car. I got something to show you."

"I don't want to, George. Let me go back to sleep."

He didn't say anything—just squeezed my arm tighter and kind of lifted me off the floor and walked me to the door.

"Let me get a blanket," I whined. Goosebumps ran up my naked arms. "Are we going somewhere?"

"No, get in the car."

He walked me down the back steps. I started around to the passenger side of the front seat, my bare feet wet from the grass and my nightgown no warmth at all. He picked me up as he opened the car's back door. I felt empty and light like there was nothing to me at all. I started crying.

"Please, George, I want to go back in the house."

"Shut your damn mouth. I swear I will kill you and all you snotty little kids if you don't shut up."

His voice was low. The words hissed like a snake in my ear. I knew he could do whatever he wanted to.

He raped me in the back seat of that Dodge DeSoto. The cloth seats smelled like wood smoke, and the upholstery scratched my face. I kicked my legs and threw punches, but it didn't make any difference. He pinned me down and held both my skinny arms above my head. His weight crushed me on the outside and inside, too. I twisted my head to the side trying to get a breath of air. I stopped crying and held my breath. I prayed that I would suffocate and die right there. I knew this was wrong, and I knew that nobody would save me. Up until that night, I thought things would get better eventually. I didn't know a lot about the world and grownup stuff, but I always pictured things being better later. After that I just thought about today. If I can make it through the day, then maybe I can make it through the night.

I stared at my bedroom window each night after that, trying to will a little crack of moonlight around the edges. No darkness, just light. That was my protection wish that never worked. I repeated it over and over as I tried to fall asleep at night. Then, "Please, God, don't let George come tonight." But he did.

Now came the hard part. Getting rid of old dead George. That was how I was going to think about him from now on—old dead George. It had a nice ring to it. Kind of made me smile when I said it nice and slow—old dead George.

First of all, he hadn't come down into the gully like I wanted him to so I could roll him over onto the tarp. I had hidden part of a canvas tarp there in the gully, and my plan was to roll him onto that, cinch up the sides real tight, and get him into the car trunk. Sad to say, I hadn't planned that as well as the shooting. I drove the car down the road and across the fields as close to the body as I could. I was a little anxious about getting old dead George out of the open field now. I spread the tarp out and tried rolling him onto it. I nearly panicked then. Boy, was he heavy. Dead weight, I thought, and then got the giggles. My heart was pounding, but I knew I had to get him into the trunk. I finally got him wrapped up and had him sitting against the trunk.

I could not figure out what to do next. There was some blood on the ground, and the grass was trampled down where I had rolled and pushed him. I thought I might have to roll him back down to the bottom of the gully and leave him there. Then I saw a piece of metal hanging from the inside of the trunk where the lining was torn. I reached up and ripped the material away. There was a solid piece of metal across the middle of the trunk lid with a round eye hook in the middle. If I could get the rope tied around that and then raise the trunk, maybe it would raise the body enough for me to push it in.

After three tries, I got my knee underneath one end of George (I had no idea if it was the head or foot end) and swung him into the trunk. I threw everything else into the back seat of the car, backed up, and surveyed the scene. If it rained soon, it might be okay. Deer can make some big messes sleeping at night and rooting around. It might look suspicious, but if you were not trying to put two and two together, it might be okay.

The tires started spinning when I hit the gas. I had a weak moment. We were going to get stuck. I prayed one of only two prayers I knew: "Oh, God, please, God. Ole Buddy of mine. Don't let these son-of-a-bitchin' tires go out on me. Please—don't let the son-of-a-bitchin' red clay grab hold of these son-of-a-bitchin' tires and leave me and old son-of-a-bitchin' George here forever."

I gripped the steering wheel until sweat popped out on my forehead. Laying my head against the steering wheel, I hit the gas one more time and shut my eyes. When the tires got traction and we started out, I muttered the only other prayer I knew: "Thank you. Thank you. Thank you."

I eased the car back up to the road and started driving and thinking. Suddenly I was in Wicket, which was probably the wrong place to be. I spotted Katy on the street and rolled down the window.

"Where you going?" she hollered at me.

"Buying groceries for Mama. She's pretty bad today." Katy shook her head.

I went to the Piggly Wiggly and bought a jar of peanut butter, a loaf of bread, and wax paper, and sat in the car and made up four sandwiches. I was ready now to dump the body in Hale's Swamp, drive the car to the next town, and take the bus out of there. No, even better, I'd buy my ticket, then leave the car in a parking lot disabled some way and hike back to the bus station.

On my way to Hale's Swamp, I stopped at the cafe to use the phone. I called Aunt Flora to make certain Irene went home before suppertime so Roy would get fed. I told her I was in town with Katy, and George had stormed off mad so I didn't know if he would be back tonight or not. Aunt Flora said she would send home some leftovers and be sure Irene got home before dark.

"Thanks, Aunt Flor," I said for the five-hundredth time. She was good-hearted but knew there was just so much she could do for Mama, her younger sister. That took care of the loose ends—except old dead George.

Hale's Swamp stretched over several miles on the west side of our town, Wicket. It was between Highway 431 and Stantonville Road and covered thirty square miles. It was fed by Little Cane Creek, which was fed by the larger Como River, which snaked all over this part of Mississippi. There were lots of springs scattered over the swamp, and people said there was quicksand there. The deadening trees' dark fingers rising to the sky looked lonely and forbidding. The land was originally part of the Hale family farm. They all had died, and the name remained. Few folks knew why it was named that, and some thought it was Hell's Swamp.

Local folks used it for fishing and duck hunting. The water could range from barely negotiable in a boat to over forty feet deep. This time of year there wouldn't be anybody around unless somebody was carp fishing. The only hard part for me would be deciding where to dump the body to make sure the water was deep enough. Those areas were deeper in the swamp, too. I knew about the swamp from my older brothers' hunting there years ago. I guess I had never really thought I would get this far.

All I knew for sure was I couldn't keep driving old dead George around in the trunk. The dirt road narrowed, and I could see the place where the fishermen put in. There was an old fiberglass canoe tied up to a concrete slab. Folks had used it for so long that no one knew anymore who the boat belonged to. I turned the car around so I was headed back out toward the road. The thin sunlight of the March afternoon didn't penetrate the deadening here, and you had to look up to be sure it was still light and the sky was still blue. I watched a couple of hawks dip and glide above, looking for some defenseless rabbits, I'm sure. I turned then and jumped—a man was standing there on the edge of the woods.

Shit, I had forgotten the two old bachelor men who lived on the edge of Hale's Swamp—Mr. Hill and Mr. Hunter. They had been known to dump things in the swamp for people for a certain fee. They lived on the back side of the swamp the farthest from any road or person they could get. Talk was that one of them had served time back in the '30s for killing a man in a fight. I never paid that much attention if it was so or not, or which man it was. They both looked like they were in their eighties—rarely shaved and even more rarely bathed. They fished and trapped and stayed to themselves. I had talked with them before at the feed store, where they bought seed for their garden, and during an occasional meal at the cafe.

I didn't know if this was Mr. Hill or Mr. Hunter. He nodded his head, and I lifted my hand to him. He had on an old feed company cap with the letters so worn and dirty I couldn't make out the name. The cap shaded his unshaven face and hid his eyes. His arms hung beside his worn blue overalls, and his hands looked too big for his too-short sleeves. He hooked his thumbs behind the front bib. I found my voice and decided I better speak.

"Mr. Hill? It's Meshac Brownlow from the cafe?"

He never acknowledged if I had the right mister but walked over to me. We eyed each other.

"Whatcha doing out here?"

I shook my head. I didn't know what to say, and I didn't have a good lie ready so I kept quiet. I felt like running, but I could not even move my little finger. We stood there for several minutes. The swamp settled down around us. Every birdcall and every breeze whispered, but I could not quite tell what they were saying. Mr. Hill walked up to the edge of the water and propped his foot on the boat. I could see the name someone had written on the side—*Fishhawk*. The boat was narrow like a canoe and could make its way through shallow water. You could even drag it across the sand if you were stuck someplace. Finally I got enough nerve to speak.

"Is there really quicksand out there?"

He didn't move at first and then turned his head toward me. "Yeah."

"I'd always heard there was." My voice was carried away by a gust of cold wind. Suddenly I started shaking all over like a rigor. I couldn't stop.

He looked back out at the swamp. "You have to know where to look for it, though."

He spat a long stream of tobacco juice at the water's edge and wiped his mouth with the back of his hand.

I crossed my arms to try and stop shaking and waited. Not speaking sometimes is the best thing to do.

"You got something you need to dump?"

"Yessir."

We stood there waiting until I spoke again. "Mr. Hill, I got something you might not want to get involved with, but I sure could use some help."

My voice squeaked on the word—"he-alp." He still didn't look at me.

"I knowed your daddy when he was a kid."

"You did?" I waited another spell, and then moved to the car and opened the trunk. His eyes widened a bit as he peered into the trunk.

"You get that in there by yourself?"

"Mostly me and some rope."

"You got it wrapped up good?"

"I think so."

He never looked me in the face. "Back it up to the edge of the water and we'll see if we can git it in the boat."

I did what he said. I don't know how, but we had old dead George in the *Fishhawk* quick as a hiccup.

He pointed to the front of the boat. "I'll paddle, and you sit there. I wantcha to see where it goes."

He steered us up one way and down another till I had no idea which way we were headed. The sun got dimmer, and I tried to be still and keep my head up. One time he had to stand and push with the paddle to get the boat off the bottom. Then we came to this spot where the water looked black and deep. He paddled over it and looked like he was pulling onshore. The reeds were thicker, and it looked like there was a spring bubbling up ahead. I thought this was too shallow, but he stopped the boat. He broke off a branch and tossed it into the middle of the water about five feet away. It twirled around like a whirlpool and went down. I didn't say a word, just nodded my head. I stood up and planted my feet wide apart to stop the boat from rocking. Mr. Hill did the same.

"We need to do this at the same time," he said. "Git ready."

I picked up my end for the last time, I hoped, and when he said okay, we rolled old dead George off the side. The tarp started sinking and then floated back up to the top. It lay there still and peaceful-like for a minute. Then I saw a subtle movement to one side. Then a turn back to the other side. Mr. Hill sat down, and I kept standing there watching.

It took almost ten minutes before it disappeared. The last thing I saw was the sand riding over it like a river of velvet. I didn't feel any remorse or regret. I felt cold and numb and hungry, to tell you the truth. I sat down, and Mr. Hill paddled us back to the car. We pulled the boat up and tied it to the slab of rock. I shoved my hands into my pockets and felt I needed to say something.

"I've got some money. I'll be glad to pay you for your trouble," I said.

Mr. Hill didn't say a word.

"I know you had better things to do than help a girl sink some old rugs."

"I think ten dollars would about do it. You got that much on you?"

I went to the car and counted out two fives from my roll of money. "I'll be glad to pay you more."

"Naw. That's about all that old stuff woulda been worth, wouldn't it?"

"Probably so," I said.

He started walking off and then turned and looked at me. Touching the bill of his cap, he muttered something—Mr. Hunter. . . . At least I think that's what he said. Then he was gone.

The Way Out

The Stantonville bus station was in a seedy part of town. Everything looked gray—the building, the seats, the ticket counter, the man selling the tickets. I walked up with my baseball cap pulled low.

"Need a ticket to Tupelo."

The man was skinny and bald. He looked like either he hadn't slept the night before or he was permanently pissed off. "One way or round trip?" he said.

"One way."

His lit cigarette dangled between his third and fourth fingers. His yellow, nicotine-stained fingers pushed some keys.

"That'll be $7.50."

I handed him a twenty. He gave me back my change. Then he reached over, pulled off the ticket, and wrote in my destination.

"Bus leaves around seven tonight and should be in Tupelo by noon tomorrow." He recited by rote: "There'll be stops announced by the driver. If you miss getting back on, you'll have to wait for the next bus. No exceptions."

He hesitated for a minute, as if he wanted to ask me something, then apparently decided what the hell and gave me the ticket. He put the cigarette back in the corner of his mouth. "Next," he said to the traveler behind me.

The clock on the wall said five thirty. Six hours since I had left the house with George, old dead George.

Stantonville was a little bigger than Wicket. Two blocks from the station was a grocery store with a cluster of small stores surrounding it. There were a few parked cars in the lot. Next to Fred's Dollar Store stood an old oak tree with some gravel spread underneath. That looked like a good place to ditch the car. I backed the car into the tall grass with the nose pointing out. It was partially hidden from the traffic.

I walked over to the dollar store and picked up some gum, a paperback romance, a metal nail file, and a crossword book. I paid and stood outside the front door. As people pulled out of the grocery, they glanced this way to check for traffic. I raised the car trunk and checked again. It looked clean. As I closed the lid, I stooped to tie my shoe and pushed the nail file into the thin rubber of the back left tire. The tire began to hiss as the air slowly leaked out. There wasn't a spare tire or jack, so maybe if somebody stopped, they'd think the driver had gone for help. I tried to walk back to the station as quickly as I could. I didn't want to call any attention to myself.

I pushed open the door to Charlie's Diner directly across from the bus terminal. The diner was dimly lit and full of smoke, grease, and tired travelers. I took the first booth and waited for the waitress. The limp menus were stuck between the napkin holder and sugar dispenser. I chose the cheapest thing on the menu—toasted cheese with pickles. The waitress took my order and set down a glass of water. I wolfed down the warm sandwich and looked to see if there was any homemade pie in the glass case on the front counter. But the case was empty. Anyway, it was close to six thirty.

There weren't a lot of passengers waiting for a seven o'clock bus on a Saturday night. If I could make the first hundred miles without seeing somebody I knew, I should be all right. Things kept popping into my mind. Would the sheriff start looking for George? I told Aunt Flora that George had left mad. Would anybody find it strange that George and I were both gone? Would old dead George stay at the bottom of Hale's Swamp? Was my secret safe with Mr. Hill or Hunter? My mouth was so dry I couldn't even spit.

The door opened then, and a young guy appeared with a duffel bag slung over his shoulder. He walked like an animal, wary-like and soft on his feet. I wondered what his story was and where he was headed. Then people gathered their belongings to board the bus. I fell in line.

The bus was about half full. I edged down the aisle with my head lowered and found a seat about halfway back. I took the window seat and put my bag next to me to discourage anyone from sitting there. It worked. The bus pulled off, and I sat alone for what I hoped was the entire night. There was no one to wave goodbye to that night. I had said my goodbyes to my family many years ago, perhaps when my father died, perhaps when George took me to the car those nights. I felt no wistfulness or regret, just a sweet relief that part at least was behind me. I laid my head back on the velour seat, closed my eyes, and went to sleep immediately. I slept the sleep of the guiltless. I don't know why. Is revenge always so sweet?

I must have slept through the eleven o'clock stop. It was one in the morning when I awoke suddenly as the bus slowed down and pulled off the road. Sometime during the night, I had shifted my feet into the seat and my legs hung over my backpack with my holey socks. My head was damp around my hairline. I moved my legs and decided I better get up and move around. My stomach growled. When the bus stopped, I shoved my backpack into the top storage unit and walked into the waiting neon lights of the terminal in Laurel, Mississippi. My fellow passengers looked as tired as I felt. We shuffled across the concrete floor, blinking in the harsh light. The young guy was still on our bus. The other travelers were an assortment—a black lady with her little girl, an older white gentleman in a suit coat and hat, a couple of young women a little older than me, a middle-aged woman with a young man who looked retarded, two scruffy men with long hair. One of them had a guitar slung over his shoulder. The others blurred into ordinary people.

I got a Dr. Pepper from the vending machine to have with my sandwiches on the bus. After a restroom stop, I climbed back on the bus. There were new passengers, and I moved my backpack and myself back a couple more rows. The boy came on last and asked if he could sit next to me. I said yes.

The silver bus shifted gears as it started down the highway. The diesel fumes drifted up and hung in the back of my throat. I took a quivery breath. The lights of Laurel faded, and I could feel the vibration from the loose gravel road as tiny sparks of light pinged against the mud flaps. The hum of the wheels matched the speed of the night. I dropped my head back against the cushion.

George taught me a lot—how to hate, how to watch my back, how to trust no one. He taught me all about revenge—that bloody, eye-for-an-eye, tooth-for-a-tooth revenge. I learned about patience, perseverance, and fate on my own. He raped me seven times that spring. Seven. Each one more horrible than the last. Death would have been a welcomed friend. Then all of a sudden, it stopped. I don't know why. I don't know if somebody threatened him or if the Lord got a hold of him or what. He still lived in our house, and still looked at me, but he never touched me again. But I still remembered every single time. I never forgot. Sometimes when I closed my eyes, I could feel my heart start to race, and the smell of him would well up in my nostrils until I felt sick.

I thought for a moment the guy next to me said something, but when I looked at him, he was perfectly still with his eyes shut.

We rode like that for a couple of hours, and then the bus made a stop at Bison. He stood up in the aisle to stretch, and I moved out of the seat and into the station. Only a few passengers got on, and when I returned to my seat, I spoke to him. My voice skipped as I spoke. He had to stoop a little to hear me.

"I've got a radio if you don't mind the music. It doesn't matter to me either way."

"Fine with me," he said.

I balanced the radio on my right thigh. Tuned in to WJMS, the music drifted in and out of my head all night as I slept, awoke, nodded, and watched the darkness. The music beat in time with the hum of the tires and bumpy back roads of Mississippi. I fell asleep to Elvis crooning, "It's Now or Never."

There was something reassuring about riding next to this guy on the dark bus. I don't know why, but I felt comforted by his nearness. His name was Billy, and that's all I knew about him. I woke up refreshed at the next stop. Billy was going to Memphis. I had begun to think that I ought to change my route once I got to Tupelo in case someone was following me. There was a large map of Mississippi hung there next to the pay telephone. I was studying it when this creep walked up behind me. He was short and bald with black, bushy eyebrows and no chin. His clothes hung off him like a dirty dishrag. He rocked back and forth on his feet.

"Know where you're going?"

I didn't turn around. He stood there breathing on me. The door of the men's restroom opened, and Billy came over. The old man walked off. I studied the map some more. I could see where the Natchez Trace bisected the upper corner of Mississippi. Tupelo was near the Tennessee border.

Billy said, "I've still got a ways to go. How about you?"

I decided then before I spoke that I should be getting out once I got to Tupelo.

"You got somebody in Tennessee you going to see?"

"No," I said.

We both stood there looking at the map.

"Why did you think I was going to Tennessee?"

"Just assumed, I guess." He crossed his arms and stood there a moment before he turned and walked off.

I thought I better shut up then. As the bus pulled out, the sky seemed lighter out the window to the east. At least the night didn't look quite so dark. I closed my eyes, but I couldn't quiet my mind enough to sleep. Suddenly the sun came up, and went from a boiling red to yellow in a few minutes. Daylight always made me feel better. My behind was tired of sitting. I was ready to move around and have a real meal before I started the next part of my journey. I did hate to say goodbye to Billy, though.

After about a hundred more stops, the bus finally pulled into Tupelo. We had a two-hour layover before the next bus to Memphis left. Most of the passengers I had left with had changed into other people or disappeared. The weird little man was gone. There seemed to be more white faces here in Tupelo than there had been coming through the rural part of Mississippi. Black faces seemed to be the same to me, though. All of this talk about segregation and integration felt like it affected somebody else, somewhere else. There was a knot of people gathered around a TV there in the terminal lounge. I stood on the outside of the circle and saw pictures of people running and the police and some black man making a speech. All the people watching were white people, of course. Somebody said something, and the others shook their heads and wandered off. I wasn't too interested in that black-white stuff. I wanted to be sure that some fool wrapped up in a tarp hadn't made national headlines down in Wicket, Mississippi.

After I freshened up, I met Billy and we had a real meal in the cafe next door. I told him I had decided to stay overnight in Tupelo and go on to either Memphis or Richmond to see my older sister. That popped out of my mouth like things do sometimes. He didn't blink, so I guess it sounded like the truth. It really didn't matter what he thought, though. I enjoyed that meal. It was kind of like a date. We talked and laughed and flirted a little. It ended when we ran out of safe things to say. Thank God he didn't say something like, "Maybe I'll see you again." Billy said goodbye, and I walked down the street toward downtown Tupelo.

It was a good-sized town. There were several restaurants—one of which had a "help wanted" sign in the window. An old but respectable-looking three-story hotel on the square had a vacancy and advertised weekly rates. There were also a couple of drugstores chock-full of goodies—a magazine stand, a candy counter with salted cashews rotating under a heat lamp, and a soda fountain. I wandered in and asked the pleasant older lady behind the counter, "Is there a place to stay for a few days here—not too expensive?"

She tucked her chin and looked at me over the top of her glasses. Her white hair was neat, and she wore a retractable pencil pinned to her ample bosom. "Hotel Tupelo, right there." She waved toward the building I had seen. "It's old, but it's clean. Looking for work or passing through?" She eyed my bags and slept-in clothes.

"Maybe both." I smiled as warmly as I could. I couldn't tell if she was one of those do-gooders or just nosy.

She prattled on, "I'd try the hotel, and then they're hiring at the sewing factory on the other side of town for the third shift."

"What about the cafe over there? Do they want a waitress or a cook?"

She looked at me a little oddly. "I don't know, but Velma is the one to talk to over there."

I thanked her and paid for my Chocomints. I put a mint into my mouth and walked over to Hotel Tupelo to see about a room.

There was a big porch that ran around three sides of the hotel. Rockers and chairs were scattered across the porch, and big, empty pots sat beside two porch swings. The floor creaked comfortably as I walked across and opened the double front door. The cigar smoke was strong but not unpleasant. For a Sunday afternoon, the lobby was quiet and still. Chairs and couches lined the large, square room, and an older man sat at the wooden registration desk, his head resting on his hand as he read the Sunday paper. I approached the desk, and he kept reading. As he turned the page, he let his eyes wander over me and said, "Can I help you?"

"What's your rates on a room?"

"Single or double?"

"Single."

"How many nights?"

I shifted my bag slightly. "Is it cheaper the longer I stay?"

He looked up at the clock on the wall. "One night is four dollars. Three nights ten dollars, a week twenty dollars."

"I'll take three nights." I leaned against the desk.

"You twenty-one?" He was daring me to say no.

"Sure," I said and tried to smile an adult smile.

He shoved a register in front of me. "Sign here. Got any bags?"

"Just these." I started to write Meshac and then decided my name should be Melinda. Then I realized he might ask for identification, so I made it Melinda Meshac Browning. I dug in my bag for my money.

"To get the rate for three, you need to pay for all three at once." He turned the register back and inspected my signature.

"That's fine." I handed him one of my well-worn twenties. He made change and handed me the key.

"Need any help?" he said without moving a muscle.

"Nope. I can make it fine. Thanks." I found the staircase and walked up to the second floor.

The room was small but clean. The bedspread was a little threadbare but better than home. I filled the big, white tub with water and climbed in. I ran the water as hot as I could. I must have been dirtier and more tired than I thought. Soon I was dreaming 'bout Mr. Hunter and that clammy tarp with old dead George. His face kept bobbing up from the top of the whirlpool, and the quicksand whirled around faster and faster. He wouldn't stay down, and Mr. Hunter and I had a long pike pole jabbing at his head trying to push him down. The water was whirling faster and faster, and George looked like he was about to shoot out of there like a rocket.

When I woke up, the water had cooled down and there was a grimy film on top. I stood up, drained the water, and then stepped in for a hot shower with lots of soap. I washed my hair with the bar of soap and at last stepped out and felt clean. I didn't know how long that feeling would stay, but now I felt pretty good. When the pictures started again, I would think about something else. What that would be, I didn't know for sure. I pulled on some clean underwear and a sweatshirt, pulled back the covers, and went to bed like it was the middle of the night. If I dreamed anything, I don't remember it. When I woke up, it was turning dark outdoors. Outside my window, two cars moved around the square. The restaurant lights across the street beckoned. I got dressed to go have supper.

It was nearly eight o'clock when I walked into the Town House Restaurant. It was practically empty since it was a Sunday night. I walked to the back corner table as soon as I got a nod of approval from the waitress. She was busy with a couple of booths near the front. The menu was on the table with the daily specials. For Sunday it was chicken and dumplings, greens, butter beans, baked apples, bread, and tea for $1.25. Although it was late, I hoped there was still plenty. The waitress appeared in her pink uniform with one of those fancy starched handkerchiefs on her shoulder.

"Is it only you or are you waiting for someone?" She set a glass of water on the table.

"Just me."

"What'll it be then?"

"Is it too late for the special?"

"Nah. We've still got plenty, I'm sure."

"I'll take the special with sweet tea."

I laid the napkin out on the table and tried to relax my shoulders. They were hunched up to my earlobes. As I looked around, I tried to avoid anyone looking my way. There was a large calendar on the wall from the Yum Yum Gin Company, a clock advertising Page Jewelers, and an aluminum hat rack near the door with forgotten hats and caps piled on the shelf. The front lunch counter gleamed. The shiny stools lined up like toadstools waiting for the next warty toad to come hop on. The conversations were low and blended with the usual sounds of eating—forks hitting the plates, spoons stirring coffee. Everything soaked in, muted and slow, and I sat and watched and let it wash over me. Damn, I was tired, but right now it was a good tired.

The waitress brought the tea, which was cold and sweet. The outside of the glass was slippery where it had condensed setting up with ice in the bottom of the cooler. I drank half of it in one gulp, and when she brought my plate with a little basket of cornbread muffins, I thought I was going to bust out crying. It all smelled so good.

"Want me to leave the pitcher of tea?"

"Yes, please," I managed to mumble with my full mouth. I shoveled in the chicken and dumplings and chased the beans around the plate with my cornbread and fork. The greens were good—greasy and stringy the way I liked them. I even ate all the apples and was a little shocked when I reached back into the basket and realized I had eaten all the cornbread. I hadn't even taken time to butter it. I told myself I should slow down, but I didn't. Finally, I pushed back from the table and nudged the plate forward. The ice in the tea clanked against my teeth as I raised the glass to get the last swallow. Then I was staring off into space savoring the food I had devoured like a starving hyena.

"Was the food all right?" the waitress asked a little sarcastically.

We both looked at the clean plate and the few crumbs of yellow cornbread.

"Yeah, it'll do, I reckon."

She smiled and said, "We've got banana pudding."

I didn't even hesitate. "Yes, ma'am, please."

She brought it, thick and gooey with the vanilla wafers damp and crumbling. It nearly took my breath away, and I ate it slowly.

The businesses were closed. Most had tiny lights in their windows. There were maybe eight cars around the square. Nothing was moving. The air had a little kick to it. March 21? It wouldn't be long—then I stopped. I did not have to figure how long it would be till the buttercups pushed up or the forsythia started to bloom. I was starting a new life, remember? I was only interested in traveling weather. I walked across the street through the front doors of the Hotel Tupelo and up to my room.

I stretched across the cool sheets and left the bathroom light on like at home. I didn't roll over until the morning sun streamed across the bed. I could hear water running and doors banging as the traffic hummed outside. I lay awhile longer trying not to think.

When I finally faced the day, I picked a new place to have my morning coffee—a doughnut shop a block over. The smell of warm cinnamon rolls invited me in, and the coffee wasn't bad, either. Someone had left the *Tupelo Times* on the table, and I buried my head inside while I sipped coffee and listened to the talk around me. Near the front window were the older women. In the back, the farmers and other men gathered around a community table. Some customers were dressed for work. They raised their hands to others or stopped by the tables to visit.

The cook and waitress kept busy working the front counter. Businessmen came by to pick up a dozen doughnuts. The regulars waited on themselves if the counter help was busy. The waitress here was an attractive, talkative woman, probably in her late fifties. She wore her hair long and an everyday skirt and blouse with an apron. She had something to say to each customer, and that helped make the place feel real. The boss looked like he never got enough sleep. His face was hound-dog long, and he had permanent raccoon eyes. He probably opened around two in the morning to start the doughnuts. I never liked the breakfast shift on my weekends at the cafe, but some people lived to get up at five and drink coffee with the riffraff.

The local paper only had one page devoted to state news. I figured we were too far away for any mention of a missing man and girl from Wicket, Mississippi, but I scanned the front section to be sure. On my way out, I asked the waitress if there was a public library in town.

"Five blocks over that a way." She pointed behind her. "Church Street, I think. Hey, Lanelle, what street is the liberry on?"

"Church Street, where it's been for fifty years," answered a white-haired, grouchy-looking woman from the lady table.

"You planning on getting a 'liberry' card?" she asked.

"Nope," said the waitress. Then she smiled and looked at me like, "Who gives a damn, at least I'm not as old as she is." Before she could ask me anything else, I broke in with, "I'm doing research on my ancestors."

"Well, that's where you need to go. Go back to the square and walk two streets over and three blocks down. The sign is out front."

I knew I couldn't use the genealogy thing at the library because they would worry the bejesus out of me about who I was and where I was from. I was too young to be researching my roots anyway. I stopped by the hotel, picked up my backpack, and stuck some hotel stationery in the bottom with the giveaway pen and tablet. I decided to say as little as possible. The more lies you tell the harder it is to remember. At least this would give me a day of rest away from the prying eyes of the law. I could always do some good thinking in a library.

The library was in the middle of the block with huge oak trees around it. It was a nice brick building with two white rockers on its front porch. The carpet was worn, as it should be, and the front desk was under the command of an elderly lady who looked like a spinster librarian. I was shocked when she picked up a cigarette from the ashtray next to her and took a long drag as she looked at me.

Her offer to help was sincere, but I sidestepped her curiosity by heading straight to the reference section. I found the most secluded area and settled in with my notebook and pencil. Business soon picked up at the desk, and after about an hour, I wandered through the stacks until I came to natural sciences. I wasn't looking for anything in particular, but it felt good and reassuring to be here in this library surrounded by books and silence. I felt safe, like I could breathe again. For the rest of the day, I read and burrowed into the caverns of that old, musty book-a-torium.

About three o'clock I raised my head and found a pair of eyes looking straight into mine. He was a little man with white hair combed straight back, big ears, and no teeth. He held a *Field and Stream* magazine in his lap but didn't even pretend to be reading it. I looked back. I don't think I nodded at him. Then I waited a few minutes and went back into the stacks. I peered through the shelves to see if he had moved. He sat there waiting and staring at my empty chair. I circled around the other sections and went to the second floor with the fiction. I tried to concentrate on book titles as I walked past. When I returned, he had not moved. For all I knew, he had seen my picture on the morning news shows. I gathered my papers and re-shelved my books. When the librarian was distracted, I walked quickly to the front door and left.

There were several Victorian-style houses in the neighborhood, set back from the streets. I thought I saw someone duck behind the boxwoods that graced the corner lot of the last big house. I put my head down and walked quickly toward the hotel. Once I got to the downtown area with other people, I slowed down and window-shopped. The old man from the library was definitely there. He had to be following me. I knew it. What was going on with me? Was I some kind of old man pervert magnet?

I slipped into the hotel and took the stairs two at time. My heart was pounding as I reached into my purse for my key and rattled the knob. It wasn't working. I heard footsteps on the carpet. I looked up—oh, Christ, I was trying the wrong room. I took the key out and found my room. I slammed the door after me and slid the chain lock. Crouching beside the door, I closed my eyes and hugged my legs close to my chest. I didn't hear a thing. Then I threw myself across the bed and cried long and hard into the cheap chenille bedspread. I didn't care if anyone heard me. I was scared and alone, and I didn't know what to do next.

After I cried myself out, I fell asleep and woke up to dreams of dark woods and boats and old men leering at me. It was getting dark outside, and I lay staring at the ceiling and wondering. I had taken this path not two days ago. I was sure of myself then and sure of what I had to do. Was I going to let some dried-up pipsqueak of a local crazy spook me? Remember, Meshac. Remember what it was like when George came and got you those nights. Remember what George did to you—all alone. Remember how his hand rested on Irene's young, white neck. I felt the nausea creep up my throat, and the vomit in my throat burned as I swallowed. Remember somebody had to stop him.

So what happened when my mother's boyfriend raped me, a scared little girl, in the back seat of that car? Did God see it? Did the stars reflect the light that died in my wide-opened eyes? When the light is the weakest, is that when evil is at its strongest? Does violence always beget violence?

Did the choice of one small soul in Wicket, Mississippi, happen due to that shift in the earth that spring equinox? Or was it just my impulse that made me finally pick up the gun, fire the shot, bury the body, and find the way out?

If the slight tilt of the earth on its axis creates the seasons, is it so difficult to believe that one person's actions could cause a widening ripple of violence? Maybe I am tilted, too. Tilted toward revenge, darkness, or evil? Or are we all tilted one way or another?

"I wish somebody would help," I said aloud. And then I laughed. I had started talking to myself now. Ooh whee. What was next—the loony farm? I sat up. Okay. The immediate plan was to take a bath, go eat supper, then decide what to do with the rest of my life.

The only time I had ever left Mississippi was when I was four years old. Aunt Evelyn, on my daddy's side, died and we went to the funeral in West Tennessee. The reason I remembered was we brought back her little white feist, Speedy. He loved to chase rats out of the woodpile in the winter. Us kids would stand on the porch, and Daddy would stand between us and the woodpile with his shovel. We'd holler, "Sic 'em, Speedy." That little dog would bark and run those rats out, and Daddy would stand ready with his shovel to knock them out. Speedy's tail would wag like crazy, and we would have to drag him away to calm him down. He was always proud of himself after those rat killings. Speedy outlived Daddy, but he disappeared after George came.

I thought the name of the town where Aunt Evelyn lived was something like Norse or Nance. Strange that memory would float into my brain now. Maybe it was a sign. I decided then I needed to get out of Mississippi and head toward Tennessee. Once I came to that conclusion, my insides got easy. I felt calm.

No Turning Back

Since I felt lighter, everything around me felt lighter, too. After three nights at Hotel Tupelo, I decided to walk across the border to Tennessee. My destination was Nuanz, Tennessee, where there may be some distant relatives.

As I left town, I spotted an old cur dog tied to a parking meter in front of the bank. She looked up, asking for a pat on the head, and I obliged. The sun was warm on my back, and it felt good to be outside traipsing through the woods like I used to do when I was a kid. The day passed pleasantly enough.

When I saw a barn in the middle of a field by itself, I figured that would be the best place to spend the night. I liked being away from town

with people staring at you. Out here I could cry awhile as I walked or
hum or dance a little jig if I felt like it. I even pulled my arms out of my
shirt and walked backward a piece as if I didn't have any arms at all. This
was my life, and I was going to be whatever I wanted to be—for a little
while at least—out here in the middle of nowhere.

When I opened the barn door, I wasn't even scared. It was peaceful
inside. The barn still had last year's hay in the loft and old fertilizer sacks
stacked in the crib. I found a piece of a horse blanket and threw it over
some of the hay. When the wind lifted the gap in the door and blew it
open a little wider, in walked the dog from town. She was outlined in the
doorway there with the last rays of the sun backlighting her so I couldn't
see her face that clearly. I guess she had tracked me all day. She was a
mix—maybe collie and shepherd. She had a big, fluffy tail that curled
over her back, and her fur was black mostly with patches of brown and
white on her chest and around her eyes, or was that gray? She stopped
for a moment, and when I didn't say a word, she came up to me and sat
down on her haunches looking at me.

"Well, come on in, I guess. Are you who's been following me all day?"
She didn't say a word back.

"You want to try and get a meal out of me, is that it?"

She still sat and stared at me. Then she looked off as if she had heard
a noise.

"Don't try and spook me; it won't work. Come on, and I'll see if I've
got anything for you."

I walked over to the back corner of the barn where a window was still
intact and the last of the day streamed in. As I set my backpack down,
she walked over and sat again watching me.

"I'm not going to wait on you hand and foot, you know."

I took out the biscuits I had saved from breakfast and the one piece of
tenderloin. I smeared a little meat on the top of one biscuit and handed
it to her. She took the biscuit as delicately as a little lady at the tea table,
walked a few paces away, and dropped it to the ground as she watched
me. She approved of my choice and came back for more. I abided by her
wishes.

"Looks like I've got me a traveling companion—for a while at least."

We made us a hole in the hay, and I fell asleep with my hand on top of her head.

I didn't know how long it would take me to walk to Tennessee from Tupelo. I thought it wasn't far from the state line, but I wasn't sure. The dog and I began pushing hard between communities. We walked along the highway for a while, and then when traffic picked up, we would range out into the fields and woods. This probably cost us more time, but time was not a problem to me. I wanted my money and food to hold out until I could feel safe enough to get a job and a place to stay. We tried to find old barns or outbuildings to stay in at night, and sometimes we had to sleep under tree boughs. We usually settled in before dark, and I was so glad to have the dog with me for company and warmth. It made my life feel a little bit normal. I didn't feel like a cold-blooded murderer with a dog by my side.

On the third day, I knew I had to go into town and buy more supplies and clean up a bit. We found Highway 45 again and walked along it until we came to Stockton. It consisted of two stores, a service station, and a bunch of rundown houses. I didn't have any way to tie up my dog, so I told her to stay outside while I went in. The guy perched on his high-back stool looked like a setting hen. His gray hair was slicked straight back, and his puffy eyes were set close to his hooked nose.

"Howdy," I said. He nodded his head as I stood inside the door. I asked if he sold cold cuts. He pointed his head toward the back. A stern-looking, tall woman was behind the white enameled cooler.

I asked her for a pound of thickly sliced bologna and cheese. She took the rag bologna and the block of cheese out of the case and began cutting them. I got a box of crackers and some bottles of cola. Not too many 'cause I couldn't carry them far. I still had my peanut butter, but I needed some water. I found some plastic bottles of juice with screw-on lids and added them to my stack on the counter. The woman wrapped up the meat and cheese in white wax paper and taped it closed.

As I went to check out, a couple of men came in the door.

"Ralph, whose dog is that out there?" one of them said.

"Where?"

"Out there by the mimosa tree."

"I don't know," he grunted.

The men tromped back to the counter to order their sandwiches. I didn't say a word. Ralph added up my purchases on his adding machine. It looked like it was a strain for him to raise his fat arms up high enough to pull the brass arm on the machine down.

"That'll be $2.60," he wheezed and then reached behind him for a big, long stick. I feinted to the left. He shoved the stick over my shoulder until it hit the wooden door that stood ajar and pushed it shut. He never left his seat.

Damn, I had forgotten to peel off some of my money before I came in. I reached for my roll and tried to hold it under the Mr. Tom's Peanut display. I found a ten and gave it to Ralph.

"Out of ten," he said as the cash register rang and the drawer pushed out. He counted my change flat on the counter, and I picked it up.

"Thanks," I said and then looked right in his face. There was still no expression that I could see in his beady eyes. He had fat jowls, dark bags under his eyes, and sweat on his wide, white forehead. He nodded. I picked up the dog, and we walked straight down the side of the road until we were out of sight. Then we turned and went into the fields as far over as we could to reach a stand of trees. There we ate a little lunch. I hoped we would find a pond soon for the dog. She licked some of the juice from my cupped hands.

There was a house in the distance, but I didn't think we should get too near in the daytime. We walked the rest of the afternoon in and out of woods and pastures with the road always west of me. The sun felt more like a summer sun. The backpack got heavier. I was tired of squatting in the woods, and I really needed a bath. Even a spit bath would be nice, but I felt I needed to keep pushing. Maybe walking wasn't that great an idea after all.

We stayed out two more nights. The last night we were in a barn piled high with hay. It looked like it was nearly abandoned. After we ate again, we lay with the back door open and looked out at the moonlight. There was a glow in the low part of the sky north of us, and I figured that was a good-sized town. We might have to rent a room there and clean up tomorrow and then decide how to get to Tennessee. I would have to leave the dog behind if I took a bus, and I didn't know if I was ready to do that. Hitchhiking could be a problem, too, with a dog.

All of a sudden, her fur stood straight up on her back. She growled low. I stood up and shut the door and backed her and my backpack into the far corner near the front side of the barn. If I had to run, this was level ground here, and it moved us closer to a couple of houses at least. She growled again. I patted her and shushed her. About that time a coyote howled at the moon or our scent, but my dog barked twice before I could hush her up.

We crouched there in the dark, and I thought about my room at home and old dead George's body spinning down in the swamp, and for a minute I wanted to cry out, "Come and get me. I don't care." But I didn't. I scrunched my eyes up tight until the dark turned green. And the coyotes howled again, and that was it for the night. I didn't sleep much that night, and as soon as daylight started eating away the darkness, I got up and pulled on my boots and set out.

We made it to Corinth about the middle of the afternoon, and I checked into a hotel. It was easy enough to sneak the dog in once I was settled. The lady at the desk didn't pay much attention to someone like me. After a good long bath and a hot meal, the dog and I took a walk in the twilight. Our reflections in the store windows showed a couple who were at ease with each other. She padded along with me, stopped when I stopped, and sniffed a few parking meters and the odd tree here and there. She looked at me once and whined as if she thought we should be somewhere else now that night was coming on. I enjoyed being near people and lights again, and I didn't pay her that much attention. Out of the blue, this black lady appeared on the sidewalk next to us.

"Ring, is that you?" she said.

My dog went to her immediately and climbed up onto her lap to have her head stroked.

"I thought that was you, where you been?" The woman patted the dog's head and ran a hand down her back. The dog shivered in relief and kept standing there on her back legs, staring at the old lady's face.

"'Scuse me, ma'am. Is that your dog?" I asked.

She looked at me as if I were some alien.

"I reckon it is. This here's Ring."

I said, "Ring?" When I did, my bosom friend looked back at me and came to my side, reluctantly, I might add.

"This is my dog, I'm afraid. You must be mistaken."

"No," she said, "that's Ring all right. She came right to me."

"But we're from out of town," I stammered.

"Where 'bouts?" she came back at me.

"Oh, a good way from here," I countered.

"Well, this here is Ring, and we been knowing each other for about seven years now. She came to me after my oldest daughter died."

"There must be some mistake. Do you live here?" I felt for Ring's furry head.

"Yes, I do."

"When's the last time you saw Ring?" I tried to move Ring back behind my legs.

The lady put one hand on her hip and pushed her purse to the crook of her arm. "It must have been about last October or November. We came into town, and I left her outside Mr. White's store there." She pointed up the street. "When I came out she was gone. I looked around and then went on home 'cause sometimes she would do that."

"Do what?"

"Take a little trip on her own." She looked me in the face then and nodded her head.

"Really?"

"One time she stayed gone nearly a year."

I bent down to the dog and gave her a hug. "Go on with her then, girl."

Ring knew what I was saying, for she looked at me long and hard and then turned to the woman.

"Thank you for the loan of your dog. She's a fine traveling companion."

"That she is."

Then Ring turned and walked out of my life. Stranger things have happened, but I couldn't think of anything right then to top that in the dog stories I'd heard. It was just as well to go solo from here on out.

I padded back to my hotel room, checked my backpack, and called it a night. I was just half a day's walk from the Tennessee line. For some reason, I thought it was important that I cross the border on my own. I could catch a bus into the nearest town to Nuanz once I was out of Mississippi. I woke up several times that night reaching for that familiar furry head.

The next morning was bright and full of promise. The decision to walk across the border into Tennessee still seemed the thing to do. Just me on my own two feet. I set out early following the road out of Corinth. I walked in the fields as much as I could even though the early morning dew wet my boots and pants legs. I knew they would dry out soon. I kept listening for the dog and then telling myself, "She's gone, Meshac." I missed her.

It felt good to stretch my legs and swing my arms. I always had liked walking. I figured it would take me most of the morning to get to a town large enough to catch a bus, but I mostly wanted that feeling of walking . . . under my own will. One step at a time.

The traffic was scant once the early morning workers went by. Now it was mostly farm trucks rattling down the road. I stopped for a spell underneath a big oak tree. I needed a moment to clear my head. I got back on the road and, sure enough, over the next hill was a wide place in the road—Guys, Tennessee, population 393. I had made it out of Mississippi. Weeds grew around the sign, but it still looked good to me.

I tried not to look too conspicuous as I meandered through town. There were empty buildings and a few cars and trucks. I kept my head down and prayed that nobody would look up and wonder about me. The dust was like powder and made little puffs as I plodded through Guys, Tennessee. I heard some voices and a screen door banged shut, but I just kept walking. Once I got outside of town, I veered off the road and crossed a ditch. There weren't any fences, but it looked like the land had been used for pasture. Suddenly I saw some movement out of the side of my eyes. I didn't know whether to turn and try to catch it or ignore it and hope I was safe.

Then something hit me right in the middle of my back. I turned around and caught sight of some legs dangling from a tree branch behind me. I looked on the ground and spotted a rotten walnut still in its shell. I picked it up and tossed it into the air. Bored kids, maybe? If they wanted to hurt me, they wouldn't be hiding, now would they? I held the weapon in my hand and walked on. The sun was bearing down, but I felt like I was making good time. The morning passed, and I thought I might try to hitch a ride. I walked along the side of the road until finally a car pulled over. A woman leaned her head out the window.

"Do you need a lift?"

I nodded my head and trotted closer. She was the only one in the car. I slid in and she smiled at me.

"I always appreciated a ride when I was hitching."

"Thank you very much." I held my bag in my lap.

"I'm only going into Selmer, but that might help."

I looked at her as she checked the rearview mirror and pulled out. "I'm trying to catch a bus."

"Well, we'll go right by the station."

I relaxed against the seat. The wind whistled through the windows, and she turned the radio up louder. Good, I thought, we won't have to talk. When we came into town, she pulled over.

"Two blocks over is a gas station." She pointed out my window. "The bus leaves from there."

"Sure do appreciate the lift." I eased out of the seat.

"Glad I could help out."

I found the service station. I didn't see anyone waiting on a bus, but the schedule hung on the wall. A man came from the garage side, wiping his hands on a greasy rag. "Can I help you?"

"Need a ticket."

"Hold on a minute." He hollered out the back for someone named Neasy. A short, plump woman appeared. The guy pointed at me. "She needs a ticket."

The lady pointed me over to the counter by the plate glass window. I saw a couple of chairs there. She opened her book and asked me where I was headed. The wait wasn't too long, and I sat and thought—but not too much.

The bus rolled into Jackson, Tennessee, late that afternoon, and I had to wait till the next morning to catch the bus to Nuanz. I thought it would be all right to bunk out in the terminal. I found a Coke machine and a package of peanuts. There was a young girl with her mother sitting across from me. Something about her reminded me of Irene. Maybe it was the way she constantly looked at her mother for approval. Irene did that. I would say, "Irene, buck up. You know what to do; now do it." And she would then—for a little while. Maybe I made her too dependent on me. Maybe she would get a little backbone about her now that I was gone. I needed to call home, but it was still too early.

I caught a little sleep on the hard wooden bench. Today was the third day of April, and I had been gone from home for two weeks. I felt better knowing I was no longer in Mississippi. I was anxious to see what Nuanz held for me.

The next day was full of sunshine. The breeze had warmth underneath it like spring was starting to slide into summer. Two men sat across from me waiting for the next bus. Their conversation was about something called sit-ins at lunch counters up in Nashville and Greensboro. They shook their heads and griped about how everything was getting out of control. Must've been some of that integration stuff. It was no business of mine.

Paradise Found

It was a quarter past two when I walked into Love's Launderette. Four of the washers vibrated in their spin cycle, and two of the dryers tumbled a rainbow set of clothes. I stuffed my duds into the nearest pink washing machine, poured in the sample box of detergent, and sat down in the lone wooden chair at the front window. The manager leaned against the backroom doorway. He was thin and stooped with wings of white hair and pretended not to know I was there. Forgotten wet towels molded on the folding table. The humid, warm air made me sleepy. The smell of bleach reminded me of Aunt Flora's laundry days as her Purexed white sheets flapped on the clothesline.

Edna Love founded Love's Launderette. Her portrait hung on the far wall over the detergent dispensers. "Edna Love, Proprietress," read the brass nameplate. In her day, Edna must have been something else. The lighting underneath threw a half moon of light on Edna's good side but plunged her other side into a sea of darkness. The portrait hung high on the wall locked behind a steel cage, like something you'd have a fancy painting behind in New York City. The wall around her bore the stains of disgruntled launderette patrons. A burned Playtex girdle hung from the lower corner, and stains from pink detergent and brown soda made a dim pattern around her portrait. Or maybe they had tried to steal her portrait for their own perverted reasons. But there she hung in her glorious pink cloud of froufrou and feathers. It made me wonder where else Edna's picture may have been.

"Can I get change for a dollar?" I asked the manager.

"Shoot, I reckon." He hobbled over to me, rattling the change in his pocket. His left leg was bowed out, and he balanced on a tall, built-up shoe for his clubfoot.

"Where you from, little lady? I ain't see you in here before."

"No, sir, I'm from Alabama. First time in town."

He grabbed my dollar. "Uh-huh. Here's your quarters. Don't use number twelve. It's not filling right."

He pulled the rolled-up comic book *Wonder Woman* from his back pocket and swaggered back to the doorway.

I transferred my clothes from the washer to the dryer. There were no other customers, so I decided to take a look around town. Nuanz was the county seat of this small rural area of West Tennessee. There was a court square with an old courthouse with businesses surrounding it. Lawyers, banks, pawnshops, and insurance offices skirted the downtown.

On the west side of the square was a restaurant—the Bluebird Cafe. A few pickups were parked out front. A faded bluebird flew across the front window. It should be a good time to ask a few questions without too much notice. I pushed open the heavy front door with its stickers from the Chamber of Commerce and local Elks organization. Hours were 5 a.m. until 8 p.m. There was a haze of blue cigarette smoke over the tables. The afternoon coffee break had ended, and the few stragglers left leaned over their cups and crumpled napkins. There was one waitress, so I sat on a stool at the silver and red counter. My arms stuck to the counter—spilled sugar, I reckoned—and the waitress started at me with a wet dishrag. I held my arms up while she gave the counter a swipe.

"Care to see a menu?" She peered at me through her bifocals. A twig of hair brushed against her earpiece, but she didn't stop to wipe it away.

"A glass of iced tea if you don't mind. Sweet tea."

She turned back to the tea urn and shoved the ice into the glass with her left hand as she grabbed her waiting cigarette with her right. The glass filled slowly with her left hand on the spigot as she got one good drag off the cigarette.

"Here you go."

My stomach rolled a bit as the cold tea hit it. In the mirror behind the counter, I noticed one guy at the back table. He was alone. His khaki legs crossed at his knees, and his foot swung a little like a cat's tail twitching before it pounces. His eyes held mine for a long glance and then moved away.

As I finished my tea, the waitress wandered back to check on me. She didn't seem to want to talk, so I paid her and walked back to the launderette. Old Clubby was still there reading *Wonder Woman*. He clomped over to the folding table. My undies flapped in the breeze as I shook them out and folded them into a tight square.

"Gonna stay the night?"

"Might. Where could a girl stay real cheap?"

"My back room is the cheapest place around," he leered at me.

"What's my next choice?" If he only knew, I thought.

"There's one motel out on the edge of town. That a way."

I packed up my clothes, being careful not to let him see the gun in my bag. I retrieved my bedroll and other gear I had stashed behind the building and started walking north out of town. The motel was red brick with a neon sign that read: "Nuanz Motor Inn Owner: Sheriff Willard Hensley." That set me back a bit, but the vacancy sign was lit. The black maid was cleaning one of the rooms and hollered across the parking lot at me, "Be there in a minute."

I waited inside the office to see what the rate was. The black woman stepped inside. She didn't look that much older than me. Her hair was straightened, and her worn clothes clung to her. She was tall and thin with a wide smile.

"Need a room?"

"How much?"

"How many?"

"Just me."

"Single is four dollars a night and kitchenettes are twenty-five dollars a week."

I plunked down my wad of money and peeled off the twenties. My roll was getting smaller.

"Does the sheriff live here, too?"

"Yep. Him and his wife live right over there." She pointed at a separate building.

I nodded my head. "Guess I better behave then, hadn't I?"

"Guess you better not get caught."

I laughed for the first time in weeks. It felt good.

She shoved a spiral notebook across the counter at me. Not exactly Hotel Astoria. I signed my name Meshac Brownlow and left the space blank for residence. She turned it around and raised her eyebrows as her lips moved trying my name.

"Where you from?"

"South of here."

"Come in from Nashville?"

"Nope."

"They said the colored people was trying to eat at the lunch counter in those department stores up there. Lotsa trouble."

I shrugged.

She turned for the key. "My name's Loretta. I live on the back side over there. Let's see. Number 404. That's a nice number, isn't it?"

I picked up my bag. "Let's see if the room's nice to go with it."

"It is. I cleaned it myself." She walked around the desk.

"On your hands and knees?" I tried to look serious.

She came right back at me. "Sure did. How'd you know?"

"'Cause I'm as full of bullshit as you are." I grinned.

Loretta laughed and slapped her leg. She led the way to Number 404, across the drive to the middle of the first building. The dark green door looked newly painted, and she handed me the key as I threw my things onto the bed. Home sweet home, I thought.

My laundry was still warm, and I unpacked my bag and placed my meager belongings in the dresser drawers. The kitchenette was a hot plate, an old refrigerator, and a coffeepot. There was salt and pepper and one plastic plate and a fork, though, and it was clean like Loretta said. I nudged off my shoes and stretched across the bed. Here I was in Nuanz, Tennessee. I had a roof over my head for a week. The gun was stowed in my bag underneath the bed for now. If I played this right, the sheriff should not be suspicious.

I looked at the table, and the tiny calendar there said April. I could settle in here for the summer. See if I could get a job. Be real quiet and real still for a few more months before I started looking for any kinfolks. Stay to myself and keep my head down in case George popped up and people started looking for me. I rolled over on the bed, closed my eyes, and the next thing I knew the strong light of midmorning was shining through the cheap curtains. I had slept all night in my clothes.

After I showered and stepped out of my room into the sunlight, the warmth startled me. It was only April, but it felt like the start of summer already. I always loved April at home. Seemed like it made people kinder, too. Happier maybe. I thought about my mama and my little brother and sister and felt my throat tightening up. Whoa, I wasn't expecting that at all. Better get busy.

Loretta was not in the office, so I walked up to the town square. There I saw two people who changed my life, although I didn't know it at the time.

"Hello," she said. She couldn't be more than ten years old. "What's your name?"

"What's yours?" I shot back.

"My name's Grace Nell Robinson."

"That's nice."

"What's yours?" she insisted. I kept walking. "Where you going?"

I turned around and looked at the tow-headed, skinny kid. She was dressed in somebody's cutoff blue jeans, a T-shirt that was too little for her, and old, scuffed Keds. Her sun-bleached hair was a rat's nest. Her thin arms and legs stuck out like one of the Pritchard kids back home who never had milk money for school. She squinted at the sun and at me and didn't back down one bit.

"What's it to you, kid?"

"I told you my name—and it's not kid. What's yours?"

"Lucille." I looked down the street.

"Lucille what?"

"Lucille Bumble Bee."

"Is not."

"Is too." I knew this routine so well.

She walked behind me as I window-shopped in the stores and followed my nose. Finally I turned to her. "Why are you following me?"

"There's nothing else to do."

"Well, why don't you go home to your mama?"

"I don't have a mama."

I had that coming, I guess. "Well, just go on home then."

She kept walking behind me. "It's a free world."

"Sometimes it is," I muttered.

I spotted a Schlitz beer sign up ahead and turned in there to shake my little shadow. When I walked in and my eyes adjusted, I realized I hadn't picked the best place to announce I was new in town. The barmaid of Pierce's Pool Room looked at me and nodded her head. There were only a couple of patrons here this early, but the smell of cigarettes and spilt beer oozed out of the walls. The concrete floor was sticky as I made my way over to the bar.

"What can I get you?"

"Got any coffee made?"

"Sure." She poured me a cup and asked if I wanted cream.

"Nope, this is fine." I sat for a few moments before I started with my questions. "Know anywhere I could get work?"

The second person I met that day sat at the end of the bar. She looked vaguely familiar. Her companion was an older man with thin hair and gray stubble on his chin. She asked me what kind of work I could do. I told her I had worked in a lumber mill and a feed store and waited tables.

"How old are you?"

I instantly added three years to my age. "Twenty." She didn't bat an eye.

She sat there for a moment. "Tell you what, hon. Go over to the cafe and tell them Edna sent you for that waitressing job."

"Edna?" I said. That's where I had seen her. Edna Love of the launderette in the flesh.

"That's right, honey. Edna Love. This here is Catfish Somers and that's Norma. Where are you staying?"

"Out at the motel."

"You gonna be here through the summer at least?"

"Yes, ma'am, I plan on it."

"They'll fix you up just fine," she said. "By the way, what's your name?"

I introduced myself, thanked her, and trotted over to the Bluebird Cafe. She was right. I mentioned Edna, and no more questions were asked. I started work the very next day.

After two months the Bluebird Cafe felt like a second home. I made pretty good on my tips and didn't have to dig into my savings very often. People were kind of nosy at first, but that stopped after a while. I tried to keep quiet and not be too noticeable. Nothing looked familiar here in Nuanz, and nobody much even knew my last name. I began to relax a little bit. Nights were lonely still, but I could put up with a little loneliness. My gun rested in the bottom of my bag, wrapped in newspaper and covered with my blanket from home. Then summer slid in after a rainy May, and all hell broke loose.

PART II
SUMMER SOLSTICE
JUNE 21, 1960

Two Peas in a Pod

I settled into a certain routine there in Nuanz. I liked my job and most of the customers at the Bluebird Cafe. I had a safe place to stay. The nights were long. I couldn't work up my nerve to ask Edna if I could work at her club, but she let me hang out there at night. We gradually became close friends. That's how I found out that Edna Love had her finger in most everyone's pie. It was easy to let her run things for me, too.

There was no news in Nuanz about anything in Wicket, Mississippi. I really missed Irene, but I was afraid to call home just yet. The biggest news now was the talk about integration. When the civil rights movement started rumbling in the South, people said they'd integrate the schools, restaurants, and even the swimming pools. Some young black minister,

Martin Luther King, was stirring things up. A bunch of black college
students tried to sit at the lunch counters in the big department stores
in some cities—even in the Woolworth's Department Store in nearby
Jackson. They actually wanted to sit down and eat where the white
people ate. Folks were up in the air everywhere.

The first of June began to feel like summer. I took long walks around
town and started learning where some of my customers lived. Mr.
Graves, who always left me a shiny half dollar, lived on College Street, in
one of the largest houses in Nuanz. The Lewis sisters had a yard full of
roses over on Church Street. Little Gracie Robinson lived with her Aunt
Virginia beside the elementary school playground, which was across
the street from the white high school. The community swimming pool
was behind it. This was a shortcut for me as I walked to the launderette
once a week. On opening day of the pool, I stopped and watched the
swimmers for a while.

Clearly, the pool was where the rich white folks gathered in the
summer. It had been since the '50s when it was donated to the city by
the Friedman family. They were the resident Jewish family who had also
given the town money to build the Little League baseball diamond and
the elementary school playground. The pool was built at the rear of the
white high school with the dressing rooms in the basement under the
gym, and it was a beauty, twenty feet at its deepest, gleaming with deep
blue-checked tile. Next to it was the baby pool, with a fountain in the
middle. Young mothers sunbathed and watched their children there.

Grace told me that you couldn't go swimming alone in the big pool
until you could swim across the pool on the deep side of the ropes. You
had to really swim, too. You couldn't hang onto the side of the pool or
the lifeguards would whistle you back into the shallow end. The two
lifeguards perched atop their sentry post seats, twirled their whistles,
and watched the kids. When the integration question began circulating,
everyone said the Friedmans could give the word, and the pool would be
closed or left open.

It seemed strange to watch the teenagers gathered in each corner of
the large concrete walkways that ran around the pool. Clusters of kids

sat in groups or stood in line at the diving boards. For a moment I could remember that same feeling of isolation as I stood on the outside of a fence in Wicket, looking in and wishing I could be a part. I wouldn't have been allowed in the corner section with the cool kids, not with my skinny white legs and baggy, faded swimsuit. Mama couldn't understand why I wanted to go, but it turned out Mama didn't understand much about me at all.

The popular girls' beach towels were carefully laid out with the iodine and baby oil mixtures, just like at home, and damp, creased movie star magazines scattered on top. They strolled in twos past the poor, mindless boys who then jackknifed off the high board or rocked the pool with cannonballs from the diving board. The guys dipped their towels into the pool and twirled them into tight ropes to flick at unsuspecting little kids' legs. This was a rite of summer for them, swimming in the clear blue water. The colored people wanted to ruin it all by being a part of it.

That night, ten-year-old Grace stopped by for one of her frequent visits. She and I had become friends of a sort. I could relax around her, and she needed somebody to pay attention to her. There were two weather-beaten wooden chairs outside my motel room door. I sat there after work most nights reading until the light faded. Then I would gaze at the stars and try not to think dark thoughts. I could pick out the Milky Way and the Little Dipper and watch a few shooting stars from time to time. Some nights I watched the lightning bugs and the big lunar moths gather around the streetlight on the corner. That is where Grace usually found me. Grace was a welcome relief sometimes, and she had lots of tales to tell. I liked to listen.

Grace plopped down in the chair next to me. She slumped over and sighed noisily. That was my cue to ask how her day went.

"So whatcha do today?"

"Nothin'. Same old stuff."

"Saw the pool is opened. Been in yet?"

"Nope, but that's the best thing to do in the summer."

She swung her legs and waited for my next question.

"Is the water cold?"

"Freezing at first. But I get used to it."

"Do you go every day?" I was only half listening.

"Most every day. In the mornings I go to the summer program at the playground. Mr. Culp's in charge."

Mr. Fred Culp was one of my regular customers. A high school teacher, he came by the cafe every morning and ordered the same thing—a short stack of pancakes, lots of syrup, and a large sweet tea.

"Mr. Culp is real nice to us little kids. He makes sure we get picked on a team, but sometimes he gets mad and his face gets really red."

"Well, you can't blame him for that."

"No, I guess not." She leaned forward and set both feet on the ground. "Then in the afternoons I go swimming if Aunt Virginia will give me a quarter."

I nodded. I thought maybe she was ready to push off, but she leaned back and drew her skinny legs up under her. She prattled on as if we were best buddies sharing secrets.

"You know my friend Noah. Me and him go swimming there at night sometimes."

"Noah, your little colored friend?"

"Yep. He's not as good a swimmer as I am, but he's pretty good."

"Grace, you know he's not supposed to be swimming in the white pool."

"I know. That's why we sneak in at night."

I didn't say anything. My index finger was numb from marking my place in my closed book. I opened it and dog-eared the page.

"What's the matter? Do they think his black's gonna come off in the water?"

I didn't know exactly what to say. I mumbled something about that's not a good thing, and you might get into trouble. Of course, trouble is her middle name.

"Oh, one day last summer me and Noah was hanging on the fence watching the big kids swim, and Mr. Woods, the crossing guard, sneaked up behind us."

"Really?"

"He wanted to know what we were doing there. And I told him, 'Nothing.' And he looked at me and said, 'You better go on home.' And I said, 'Come on, Noah, let's go,' and Mr. Woods said, 'I'll take care of him,' and I said, 'Run, Noah.' And he did."

I felt like I should say something like a responsible adult would say, but all I said was, "You and Noah better be real careful."

"Nothing's gonna happen to me and Noah. We're like two peas in a pod." She crossed her arms and glared at me. I didn't want to prove her wrong, so I shut up.

"Well, I gotta make my rounds now," she said, but she kept sitting.

"What rounds?" Like a catfish, I took the bait.

"My nightly rounds checking up on things and people."

I got the feeling I didn't need to hear this, but I knew it would be intriguing. I encouraged her.

"Where do you go on these nightly rounds?"

"Well," she settled back, resting her head on the back of the chair and looking up at the stars. "I love being out at night when so many people are inside sleeping. It feels like it's just me and the moon and the stars. The grass gets wetter, and the trees make sounds that don't even scare me."

She looked straight at me then. "That's how I know so much. I can be really quiet and really little. It's like spying on people, but I don't look if it's something I shouldn't be seeing."

"Yeah, right."

"But spying made me think different about people. Like Mrs. Overall on Lombardy Lane. She was this old, orange-haired woman who drove this old car and was always tooting her horn at everybody. She would wave at me like she knew me. Then she'd go down the street and pick up some other old women. The most fun I had spying on her was on Saturday and Sunday nights. That's when her boyfriend came over. He was real old, too. The windows on her house cranked out, and if a breeze was blowing, the curtains would blow out and I could see them inside. They rolled the rugs back, and the furniture was catty-cornered, and they'd play records and dance up a storm. Sometimes he closed his eyes, and she hummed along with the song in one of those quivery voices. Then they'd stop and have a glass of something and rest awhile and then go at it again."

"Well," I said, "I guess there's no harm in that but . . ."

She repeated along with me with that little smile of hers, "You'd better be careful."

I smiled, and that encouraged her.

"But I liked her better after that. Me and Noah went different places, too. I know, I know. Some people would make a big deal out of a colored boy being in their backyard."

I wasn't going to touch that. Maybe if I opened my book up she would get the hint.

"Noah likes to go see the cat man."

I picked up my book and ran my thumb over the cover.

"The cat man had three cats, Topsy, Turvy, and Milkweed. In the summertime he put his cats up in the windows so they'd catch bugs for him. One night when they were scratching at the screens, Noah and me started meowing." She giggled. "The cat man came and looked out the window, but the cats didn't pay us any mind at all."

Without even taking a deep breath, she plowed on: "Of course there are some places I know I shouldn't go, but I make myself go to get used to not being scared. Like Rem's Place—where the coloreds hang out down in colored town. On weekends they have music down there. Me and Noah can hide underneath a bush and can't anybody see us at all. When I see them in the daytime—Sun Man, Boy Blue, Lottie, and Hoodlum—they seem different from the nighttime. The white people go to the River. It was scarier, but sometimes it was funny how two guys might come out and try to fight, and if nobody came out to watch, they'd go back inside. Mrs. Dorothy runs that place."

My head was swimming with this chatter from my little friend. "Whew, you are wearing me out, girl." I opened my book.

She laughed, jumped up, and with a wave of her hand was gone.

Midsummer's Eve

As the summer solstice neared, I felt it in my body. We were about to have the longest day and the shortest night of the year. Fairies and spirits and magical things hovered around us near the solstice. Things had been wild lately. First was the stabbing at Rem's Place. The police closed them down for a few nights so things would settle down. Then a white woman went missing, but people didn't seem too upset about that. The planets were lining up, and I had no idea what to expect. I toed the line at work.

On Midsummer's Eve, the night before the first full day of summer, I sat outside alone after work. The cicadas hummed and lightning bugs lit in the field beside the motel. It reminded me of nights at home when we would play "kick the can" and run and hide long after darkness had fallen. Mama usually called us in, but we already had mosquito bites and welts from the bushes we ran through in the woods trying to sneak up on the others and get home free.

I always felt like I was Daddy's favorite child. He'd look at me sometimes when my brothers made me cry or Mama would get onto me and shake his head real slow-like. Later he'd hug me when nobody was watching. Once he gave me a good-luck charm, a four-leaf clover pressed on a key chain. He said that had helped him out for a long time, too. I always felt safe when he was around. I wonder sometimes how my life would be now if Mama had died first. Summertime was made for kids. I missed it. It felt different here in Nuanz.

I had come inside and was asleep when something woke me. Sirens screamed past the motel. Their red lights played on the wall over my bed, and my heart raced as I sat up. I was disoriented, and the sirens were so loud I thought they must be outside my window. Were they coming for me? When I heard the second siren, I got up and looked out. A stream of emergency vehicles whizzed past the motel. Ambulances, volunteer firemen, pickup trucks with red lights whirring on their dashboards—all flew past the motel toward the square. I pulled on my sweatpants and walked out the door. Loretta stood in the driveway. We walked toward the street.

"What's going on?"

"Who knows? I ain't never seen that much go anywhere in Nuanz."

Then Grace ran square into me in the parking lot. Her eyes were huge, and all she could say was, "Hurry—up at the pool."

Grace pulled on me, and we ran the best we could down College Street and through the shortcut. Before we even got there, I could see the lights and cars and trucks parked harum-scarum up and down the street leading up to the high school. I saw Mr. Culp and Lawyer Malone and the Porter family with their kids in their pajamas. There were eerie outdoor lights set up and yellow crime tape all around the pool. People kept walking up and standing in groups talking low. The sheriff and his deputies were huddled together, and Chief Gray with the fire department stood over by the concrete stairs. Nobody wanted to look, but nobody wanted to leave, either.

Grace stood leaning against the chain-link fence with both hands hooked into the openings. Tears streaked her dirty little face. I stood beside her and didn't say a word. When she laid her head on her hands, I couldn't help but lay my hand on her back for a moment.

"He was my friend," she whispered.

"I know."

"We've been in here lots of times at night. He knew how to swim."

I patted her on her back.

"Did somebody shoot him?"

"I don't know, Grace. I just don't know."

I stood there as long as I could. Grace squatted down on the ground and kept staring at the pool. Lawyer Malone walked over and tapped me on the shoulder. We walked a few steps away from Grace.

"Chief said when they got here the little boy was floating face down fully clothed. They thought it was an accidental drowning at first."

I nodded my head. Mr. Malone looked strange without his coat and tie. He was pale, and his hair needed combing.

"It's Noah. You know Grace Robinson's little colored friend."

He nodded his head and said, "Yeah, they said she . . ."

We heard somebody hollering. A young black man came running up the hill.

"Somebody lit a cross in front of Mount Zion Colored Church." His eyes were huge, and he stood there waiting for someone to do something. Mr. Malone went over to him and motioned for Chief Gray. Suddenly the chief and the rest of his crew jumped onto the idling fire truck and took off toward East Side. Some of the men followed in their trucks.

I could hear the radios squawking at each other while the police stood in their tight circle by the pool. A young couple came and stood beside us at the fence. The man looked at me and said they had identified Noah's body and had gone to get his grandmother. I knew Noah belonged to the Johnson family, a prominent black family in Nuanz. His grandmother was known as Mother Rachel. Noah's mother had left him here for Mother Rachel to raise. She probably had no idea he was even out of the house when they came to ask about him.

We stood for a long time there by the pool. The water was dark as night and cold. The deputies stood back for a moment, and you could see the little mound of white sheets over by the gate.

I heard someone say, "Here comes Virginia." We turned and saw Grace's Aunt Virginia coming up the hill toward us. She walked with those long, step-over-the-rows footsteps of hers. She grabbed Grace's skinny arms and shook her. Grace began to scream, and I thought her aunt was going to slap her when the child fell to the ground in a dead faint. We carried her to the back seat of the nearest police car and stretched her limp body across the old, cracked seat. Aunt Virginia leaned against the back fender of the car with her arms crossed. Her cigarettes soon made a haze of smoke, which hung around her like a gray veil. I stood watch over Grace as the police tried to clear the crowd. No one wanted to leave. It was as if they knew something else might happen, and they didn't want to miss it.

Grace came to and sat up. I leaned in the window and asked, "Are you okay?"

"He's dead, isn't he?"

I nodded my head.

"It's my fault. I was the one who said we needed to meet up here tonight and go swimming."

"Honey, there's no way on earth this could be your fault. Poor little Noah crossed the path of a mean person—that's all."

Aunt Virginia brought her a cold, bottled Coke, and Grace drank it all down in one gulp. Then the tears started. About that time Noah's grandmother, Mother Rachel, walked through the crowd. I could hear her wailing. That's when I had to leave.

About five in the morning, there was a knock on my door. It was Grace. I let her in, and we didn't say a word. She curled up next to me and was out like a light.

As for me, it seemed death was following me around like a raggedy old petticoat. I thought everyone could probably look at me and see old dead George's blood on my hands. I get into town and this sweet little black boy drowned in the swimming pool. Is the world full of violence—waiting to bubble up to the surface?

After that night, I tried to be a little nicer to Grace. That was a big mistake. She acted like she owned me after that. I soon found out that Aunt Virginia was more than happy for Grace to spend lots of time with me. Maybe I felt like I was making up for some of my past sins; I don't know.

The next few days, talk at the cafe was all about the murder and Grace and Noah. It was unusual for Noah and Grace to even know each other, much less be friends. They went to separate schools. Noah didn't live on Grace's farm, nor did his parents work for her parents. Both kids were on their own a good part of their lives. Lawyer Malone knew the Johnson family. He sat at the front table and told all listening ears how Mother Rachel came to take care of little Noah.

"I used to do some legal work for Mother Rachel's husband, Alvin, now and then. He had some trouble with one of his brothers over some land years ago. Alvin always paid his bills, but this brother of his was worthless."

One of the men asked, "Is he the one who had that produce stand out on Bluff Road?"

Malone nodded his head and leaned over on his elbows. "Yeah, that was Alvin. He was a hard worker. They had four or five children, and this child belonged to their youngest daughter. She came home for Alvin's funeral and left the boy here when he was just a baby."

The other men shook their heads. I circled the table with a full coffeepot. I extended it and raised my eyebrows as each of the regulars either nodded yes or waved me away.

"She was good to him, but she is old—couldn't have known what all he was up to." Mr. Malone sat back in his chair and checked the time on the clock over the counter.

Then one of the Lewis sisters at the women's table piped up: "Well, Grace didn't stand a chance herself. She never had a friend her own age. Her daddy was long gone, and her mama went somewhere out west. She came to live with her Aunt Virginia, my backyard neighbor. We all know what Virginia's problem is."

No one said a word, but the coffee cups were still. They didn't want to miss something.

"Yep, never had little girl clothes, baby dolls, or tea parties. Just on her own most of the time," Miss Audrey chimed in.

I knew how much Grace was on her own and how much she loved Noah. That was a big thing because Grace didn't seem to have much love in her at all. But I kept my thoughts to myself.

Mr. Graves leaned back in his chair. "I heard he was hit in the head before he was tossed in the pool."

There were murmurs of "Yeah, that's what I heard." Then Mr. Biggs, who rarely opened his mouth, piped up, "Well, I heard the coloreds was trying to integrate the pool and done it themselves."

Everybody got quiet. I thought, "Who's going to believe that crap?"

"Well, mark my word, that black minister, Preacher Doaks, is asking a lot of questions," Lawyer Malone continued. "You know he went to one of those black colleges. He thinks he's a little bit better than the other Negroes around here." He blew on his coffee before he took a sip.

All the black-white talk kept gnawing at me. That black preacher, King, made a speech last week in Nashville. I watched it on TV. He said something like, "Do what you want to us, but we can wear you down." What was it? Something like, "We will wear you down with our capacity to suffer." Here was a heavy dose of suffering right here in Nuanz. This scared the bejesus out of us.

Grace kept coming to my motel room whenever she could. I decided to let her talk. Sometimes I could still hear her voice as I finally drifted off to sleep in Room 404 at the Nuanz Motor Inn.

Homegoing

The funeral was on the following Saturday, and Edna informed me that I would be going with her and Aunt Virginia and Grace. I had never been to a colored person's funeral, much less one for a poor little boy drowned in a swimming pool. I dreaded it, but I knew I had better do what Edna said. Besides, I felt sorry for little Gracie.

Edna picked me up last in her long, white Cadillac. Aunt Virginia was already in the front seat, smoking, so I climbed into the back seat with Grace.

The black funeral home was owned by the Simon Field family and had been around for a long time. It was in the middle of colored town. Surrounded by sagging cypress trees, the house rose up on its haunches like a fine white horse. The upstairs was the family quarters, and the downstairs was the funeral parlor and chapel. The tall columns on the front porch framed a huge door, which was opened by a light-skinned black man as we dragged down the sidewalk. The streets were packed with cars, trucks, and a steady stream of people walking in. A thick rug covered the floor, and the rooms were dimly lit. As I signed the register, I saw the sheriff and a deputy standing with their hats in their hands.

We were directed to a row of folding chairs along the back wall and then asked if we wished to speak to Mother Rachel. I really preferred not to, but Edna nodded yes and pushed us all down the aisle to the front pew. Mother Rachel wore all black with a wide-brimmed black hat and flowers in her lap. When she saw Grace, she swept her up into her lap and hugged her. Grace buried her face underneath the hat brim into Mother Rachel's neck. I couldn't hear what she said, just a lot of deep breaths and sobs. Mother Rachel patted her on the back and set her feet back on the floor.

Grace stood alone with her shoulders down, and I heard her say between the sobs, "But I want him back."

Mother Rachel looked at Edna and said, "Bring her to see me later."

The white casket sat before the pulpit with a light shining from above. Mounds of flowers filled the space all around and on top of the casket. I held back with Grace as Edna and Aunt Virginia went forward. Two little girls held hands with baskets of flowers near the head of the casket. Grace and I stumbled back to our seats, and the others joined us. Grace seemed to be in a trance—all worn out from the emotions and tears. I tried to be as still and unwhite as possible, but I knew everyone looked at us as they came in. That otherness stuck out like a horn of the devil himself—as if we were pretending to be sad. As I sat there surrounded by this blackness with sweat trickling down my back, I thought of how it must feel to be the only black person in a sea of white.

Several people spoke at the service—a young woman, an elderly man, and then two young boys read poems and a teenage girl sang a solo. The pianist ran trills up and down the piano as the choir sang. Each one's voice was mellow and soothing. People continued to drift in until there was no standing room. I could see through the windows that a crowd had gathered on the lawn underneath the trees. They raised the windows so everyone could hear.

Preacher Doaks took the podium and the homegoing of Noah Johnson began. It was full of movement with the choir swaying as they sang "Amazing Grace," "His Eye Is on the Sparrow," and "I'll Fly Away." There was sadness but also rejoicing as if Noah had crossed over to a better place. Perhaps he had. Women dressed all in white were there to support those who were overcome with grief. As the keening began, Grace covered her ears and closed her eyes. She drifted off. The ushers watched over the family, ready to help those who fainted or were weakened with sorrow. When the preacher finally began his sermon, emotions were raw. You could almost taste the sadness in the air. It was dry, like ashes. Then the anger bubbled up and nearly suffocated me.

Brother Doaks paused and wiped his brown face with a starched white handkerchief. The handheld fans stamped with pictures of the Last Supper and Fields Funeral Home kept a steady metronome beat. Some shoulders swayed a bit, and feet patted the floor in anticipation. Sweat dripped from the preacher's face onto the crinkly, thin pages of the open Bible he held close to his chest. He removed his glasses and looked up at the ceiling.

"Noah Johnson has gone home."

The fans stopped in unison and then began again as the preacher's words washed over us. I couldn't follow everything he said, but I felt a rhythm to his words that were meant to soothe like a familiar chorus. The people anticipated his next phrase and help him to sound it out, loud and thunderous. He was a master. His words poured out like water from a mountain, and the men in one corner and the women in the other corner padded the phrases with *amen, yessir preacher, uh-huh, that's right.* The fans beat a steady, relentless refrain and whispered secrets that my white ears could not understand.

Preacher Doaks began his summation, and every word hit straight at my heart:

"Noah Johnson has crossed over now at an early age. But we must remember that God is good. We must remember that some worlds are better than where we are now. Long, long ago when God created this earth, He made the land, the sky above, the ground beneath us. Man was not made from animals, but in the image of God. You see, God pushed up the earth and made the mountains rise in the east, and then He took His hand and scooped out the earth so the river could run through it. That river that carries life and a way out. That river that cuts its way through the hard rock and tangled undergrowth thick with brambles and thorns so difficult sometimes for us to follow. Oh, yes. That water that gives life and takes it away. That water that quenches our thirst and sustains our tired bodies. Little did that vile person know that the water that became young Noah's grave comes from the same God who began it long ago. That river that runs through it. Sisters and brethren, listen to me: Sometimes it's an easy ride; sometimes it's filled with danger, but God is there waiting on the other side for us. Noah is there, too."

The ushers floated down the aisle and helped Mother Rachel to her feet. The rest of us stood as the tiny casket was carried up the aisle. The women stood beside Mother Rachel and fanned her with their brown hands holding her steady as she swayed and slowly followed the casket outside. We stood together in a huddle, and the sheriff came over to talk to Aunt Virginia and Edna. I hung back.

"We need to have another talk with Grace."

"Why ever for? She's talked to you once."

"The preacher and those Negro lawyers from up north are wanting to ask her some questions themselves."

We just stood there. Then Edna turned to leave, saying, "Call me."

We shuffled into the car, and no one said a word all the way home. I was exhausted and flung myself across the bed when I finally got to my room.

How many times can a heart be broken? Does evil exist everywhere?

I wasn't much help to little Gracie in the following weeks. I kept remembering how I felt when I was her age—all alone, no daddy, and that rat George doing those things to me. It wasn't fair that Grace had to lose that little Negro friend of hers—her only friend. I soon became the substitute. That was all right. It wasn't like she was interrupting any torrid love life anyway. I tried to eke out a string of ordinary days after the funeral. Get up, go to work, come home, go to sleep, and do it all over again. I kept pushing the anger down inside of me. The only problem was Grace. She had the ten-year-old's vision of what was right and what was wrong and didn't know to leave well enough alone. She kept asking all the questions that none of us wanted to think about and certainly didn't want to find the answers to.

I wasn't the only one who was mad, either. The white managers at the department stores in the cities had refused to serve Negro customers at their lunch counters. They stated that they reserved the right to refuse to serve whomever they chose. Negroes were allowed to shop in their stores but not eat in their stores. Black college students all over the nation began to organize and put into action these so-called nonviolent demonstration methods. It looked like pure torture to me. They called it a sit-in, and it was going big time not too far from us.

Those pictures of the demonstrators at Woolworth's in Jackson wore on me. It hurt to look at them. The young people, some of them about my age, were sitting there while these hate-filled white people mocked them, called them names, and poured sugar, salt, and mustard all over them. The white people even put their cigarettes out on the demonstrators' backs and laughed as they poured hot coffee on them. All the young black men and women sat facing the counter. Their backs were ramrod straight. Their hands stayed folded in their laps. Some read their Bibles. They did not speak to each other; they never responded when people shouted those awful things at them. They never cursed or fought back. They sat and asked to be served. Violence washed over them and teetered on the edge of outbreak. Then it would stop either when the police took them to jail or the white people grew tired.

This really bothered me. It was as if we thought these people weren't human. Like they didn't breathe in and out and laugh and cry like us. Oh, I wasn't no crusader. But I wondered how they could do that. How could the demonstrators endure without striking back? I never said a word at the cafe when everybody grumbled.

"They're a bunch of troublemakers."

"They don't want to eat with us."

"They should know their place. Why would they want to come in here?"

But I cut that picture out of the newspaper and hung it next to the mirror on my motel wall. I made myself look at it every night until I could smell the mustard in their hair and feel the grainy sugar falling through their hair, into their ears, and creeping down their shirt collars. Meshac, here's a lesson for you to learn, old girl.

Resolution, Revolution, and Beyond

The Bluebird was buzzing that Monday morning in early July. We had heard that James Lovelady, the lawyer for the NAACP from Washington, DC, was coming to Nuanz. His picture on the local news showed a very black young man dressed in a brown suit, shirt, and tie. He had several men with him, all of them black and all carrying briefcases. We had never seen a black person with a briefcase before. They were in Jackson talking with the mayor about the lunch counter sit-ins at Woolworth's Department Store.

The mean talk was going big guns. I tried to listen and not even look at them. Finally Mr. Harwood said to me, "Meshac, what're you so quiet about?"

I shook my head and kept wiping the counter. The others started in on me then.

"Whatsa matter?"

"You one of those sit-in freaks, too?"

"Huh, Meshac?"

I didn't feel like kidding around with those old men, and I didn't care right then what they thought, so I gritted my teeth and made another pot of coffee.

"If they come in here, are you going to serve them?"

I finally had enough and said to the back wall, "I can pour a cup of coffee for anybody that has a dime."

The air got sucked out of the room then but, thank God, Edna Love walked in. She always took all the attention—men and women—when she entered a room. There was an uncertainty about Edna that kept you on your toes.

"Hey, kiddo," she threw back to the table of men—none of whom knew which kid she meant. They all nodded their heads or lifted their hands. A chorus of "hey, Edna," how-dos, and mumbled greetings overlapped each other. They shifted in their chairs, and Mr. Harwood immediately launched into a discussion of last night's Cardinals game.

Edna sidled over to the counter and waited while I set up her coffee for her—black. We small-talked, and then she leaned over and said low-like to me, "Those black lawyers from DC will be in town around three today. You want to go with me to meet them?"

"Why would I want to do that?"

"Because they're wanting to talk with Grace, and her aunt said she didn't want to go. I figured she'd feel better if you were there."

"What are they going to ask Grace?"

"Who knows? It's the sheriff, Noah's grandmother, and Brother Doaks."

"I don't think I can get off." (I hoped.)

"I think you can if you want to."

"Let me think about it."

She blew on her coffee and then drank it down in three gulps.

"I'll pick you up at the motel about two thirty."

She winked at me, but she didn't smile. She strolled over to the table of men and stood between Lawyer Malone and Mr. Jackson—her hands resting on each man's shoulder, lightly but with some familiarity. She leaned over and said something. They all burst out laughing like teenagers. She left with that spring in her step and never looked my way again.

Sure enough, about two o'clock, Mr. Adams came out of the kitchen and said to me, "Why don't you go on home for a couple of hours and check back in for the supper hour?"

I looked at him and shrugged. "Fine with me."

I untied my apron and hung it inside the swinging door next to the dishwashing station.

"I'll figure up my tips tonight," I hollered back at him, but he had already ducked back into the storage room.

It was so hot outside that the air took my breath away. The humidity had to be about 150 percent. I walked a couple of blocks and felt my blouse sticking to my back. As I got to the motel, Edna pulled up and blew the horn. I pointed inside my room and quickly shucked off my waitress outfit and pulled on a fresh blouse and jeans. I didn't even look in the mirror as I scooted back out to jump into the car.

"Now at this meeting you can sit there and not say a word if that's possible."

"It is," I answered.

"We'll pick up Grace and be there in case they start anything."

I didn't know if she meant the black lawyers or the sheriff, but I thought I better start practicing not saying anything. And I did. Grace and her aunt walked out to the car when we pulled up. Grace had washed her face and combed her hair. She still had on her old dungarees, but the T-shirt wasn't too faded. She was carrying a little pink plastic purse. I hadn't ever seen her with a purse before. It looked so out of place swinging there, hooked over her bony shoulder.

Aunt Virginia leaned through the car window. "I told her to not be sassy and tell them everything. If she misbehaves, you have my permission to slap her jaws."

I didn't say a word. I was practicing.

Edna said, "We'll handle everything from here, Virginia."

"Hey, squirt," I said as Grace climbed into the back seat and shut the heavy door.

Mother Rachel's house used to be white once upon a time. Its clapboard sides had faded to a nice, mellow beige, and the yard around the front porch was bare and packed hard as asphalt. I imagine you could sweep it clean. The front porch held a collection of straight-back chairs, washtubs, assorted plants, and an old cupboard full of stuff. There was a big catalpa tree in the front yard with blooms still on some of the branches. Its gray trunk was too big to reach around. There were several cars pulled under the shade of the tree—the sheriff's patrol car, a beat-up Chevrolet, and two shiny black cars with out-of-state plates.

One of Mother Rachel's sons came to the door as we got out of the car. Grace led us inside. No one spoke when we came in. The living room had low ceilings, worn linoleum, and lots of pictures on the walls. The one couch was filled with the sheriff, his lady deputy Victoria, and Mother Rachel. The other guests perched on straight chairs around the kitchen table or nestled into each corner. I didn't see any more available seats. The lawyers stood up when Edna and I entered the room. The sheriff kept his seat, of course.

"Hello, Edna," he said.

She smiled at him. "Hi, Willard."

Mother Rachel leaned forward. "Miss Edna, how you doing?" Then, "Come here, Grace."

Grace trotted over to her side. Mother Rachel hugged her for a brief moment, then turned her around to face the lawyers.

"This is Miss Grace Robinson. She was Noah's best friend."

Grace stuck her chin out and said in a loud voice, "I still am."

Everyone introduced themselves. The youngest of the lawyers then spoke to me. "And you are?"

"Meshac Brownlow. I'm a friend of Grace's."

Edna found a seat, and Grace stayed by Mother Rachel. The sheriff waited a moment and then decided he better start the ball rolling.

"We wanted to meet out here at Miss Rachel's house to have a discussion about the circumstances around Noah's unfortunate end."

I hate it when they never say what they really mean.

"Now, Gracie, these gentlemen wanted to ask you some questions. I want you to speak up and tell them exactly what you told me."

Grace stood up as if she was about to recite in school. Her hair was held back from her face with a plastic barrette that seemed to be sliding out of place. She twisted the little plastic purse in her hands, and her face turned pale beneath her tan. Her voice was soft at first, and then she dropped the purse to the floor and stood there with her eyes half-closed and her hands clenched as if she was living it all over again. I was thinking, "Go, Gracie, go." I found a corner and leaned back, watching and waiting.

"Well, it was Midsummer's Eve, you know. Meshac told me all about it. It was supposed to be a night of magic—like charms and rituals and all sorts of fun, scary stuff. Noah and me decided it would be a great night to stay up all night 'cause it was the shortest night of the year. So that was what we were going to do—meet and stay up all night."

"Did anybody else know about your plans?" asked Mr. Lovelady.

"No, sir. Not that I know of, but things were different that whole week before. Meshac said it was the stars. Everything lining up for the big shebang on Midsummer's Eve."

"What things?" asked the other lawyer.

Grace looked at me, and I nodded my head to encourage her to go on.

"Well, there was that stabbing down at Rem's on Saturday night. Boy Blue cut a man, and they had to call the law. They closed the place down for a few days, but it was the same at the River. Lots more fights in the parking lot. People were out of sorts over what I couldn't figure out." She clasped her hands behind her back and studied the floor.

"Then that thing happened over in Jackson at Woolworth's. People were really mad. But I guess you know about that."

Preacher Doaks covered his mouth with his hand, but I could see the smile in his eyes.

Grace paused long enough to give us a little breathing room and then started again. "Anyway, since we were staying out all night, the first thing we wanted to do was sneak in the pool and take a dip by the moon. That's one of those rituals, you know," she looked at me, and I couldn't help but smile back. "Dipping water by the moon on summer solstice?"

She ended the sentence as a question as if we were going to agree or
not with her statement. No one acknowledged anything.

"Had you two been in the pool before?" the sheriff asked.

Grace pretended she didn't hear and kept going.

"Noah told his grandmother he had a stomachache and went to bed."

Her eyes found Mother Rachel. "I'm sorry." Her voice softened, and
Mother Rachel nodded her head.

"We had extra clothes hid out to put on after swimming. We were to
meet at eleven o'clock underneath the water tower by the pool. I sneaked
out a little before eleven."

Grace was fine now on one of her storytelling jags.

"I climbed out my window and crawled through the hawthorn bushes
till it felt safe. The dogs next door rattled their chains, but I hushed them
up. It was Buddy and Gruff. They know me."

She shrugged her little shoulders and took a deep breath. "Noah was
waiting for me by the water tower. We knew we had to swim before the
police patrol came by at midnight. We rolled under the gate at the top
of the stairs and kept our heads down in case anyone went by. I had my
bathing suit on under my clothes, so I shed my clothes and kicked them
underneath the lifeguard chair. Noah jumped in first."

The older lawyer leaned forward and asked, "How long did you stay
in the pool?"

Grace thought for a moment. "Well, we raced to the end of the pool
and back. Then we played a game of shark."

She smiled. "Noah won. He beat me back to the ropes. So I guess
maybe thirty minutes."

"What happened next?"

"Noah wanted to go down to Rem's."

"That's Remington Moore. He runs a local club for blacks down off
the square," explained Sheriff Hensley.

Someone asked, "Why did you go there?"

"Noah said there was something big going on down there. Fire Night."

No one said a word. She had us eating out of her little girl hand.

"You know—there's a big bonfire, and the guys jump over the fire or
something. It sounded kind of neat."

There was a pause then. I spoke for the first time. "Go on, Grace. What happened next?"

"Well, we got out of the pool and let the water drip for a few minutes. Noah went around the side of the office building and put on his dry clothes, and then I did the same. We left our wet clothes underneath the nandina bushes. Then we thought we heard something."

We perked up then. The lawyers leaned up in their chairs. Edna recrossed her legs, and the springs in the couch squeaked. She bounced her leg up and down. The chopsticks in her hair seemed to vibrate.

The sheriff asked, "What did it sound like?"

"Like the door closed down by the pumps. But I don't know for sure." Grace squirmed.

"So what did you do?" I was trying to get her back on track.

"Took off running. We crossed the street, ran through the playground, and stood against Mrs. Lassiter's back wall. When it looked like everything was okay, we started walking down Church Street to Rem's."

She stopped long enough to take a deep breath. When no one said anything, she began again.

"When we got to Rem's, there was a party going on. We crawled underneath our favorite bush and watched. People kept going in and out. Cars would pull up and blow their horns, and Albert would come take their orders. Whatever they were getting was in little brown paper bags. We could hear music inside. Then Noah punched me and said, 'Look, Grace, over yonder.'

"There was a big fire in the side yard. Red sparks were flying up in the air, and people were standing around the fire adding wood. I told Noah I wanted to get closer. We crawled out Indian-style on our bellies. I think the lights went off inside. Everybody had their backs to us, but we could hear them talking."

I wanted to reach over and pat her arm, but I stayed still. I could nearly smell the smoke as her tinny voice droned on. We all were straining to hear her. Go on, sweetie. She tilted back her head and squinted her eyes as if she was there.

"Sun Man and Pee Wee took off their shirts and started strutting around the fire. The girls giggled. Boy Blue said, 'You better watch where you're going.' Somebody shoved someone nearer to the fire. We crept closer. About that time a guy in a black truck pulled up and tapped the horn twice. No one paid him any mind. Noah and me stepped back into the shadows. The man in the truck hollered and blew his horn again. Rem came out and said something to him. We peeped around the corner when all of a sudden the man turned his truck lights on. He caught us standing there. We screamed and jumped out of the way when the man drove past us. Rem came over and stared at us."

Edna asked quietly, "What'd Rem do?"

Grace looked at Edna, and she nodded her head in encouragement. Grace put her fingers up to her mouth and nibbled on her nail. Edna cocked one eyebrow and shook her head no. Grace dropped her hand back down beside her.

"Rem said to us, 'What are you doing here in the middle of the night?' We just stood there. Then he said, 'Is that you, Noah Johnson?' Noah said yessir. 'Mother Rachel's grandchild?' Noah said yessir. Rem said, 'You get your little black ass home now.' So of course Noah took off. Then Rem turned to me. 'And you, Miss White Child, who are you?' I told him I was Grace Nell Robinson. He said, 'I suggest you get home right now before I call the law for trespassing on my property.' I took off running."

No one said a word. Grace knew she had to finish the story. We waited. She looked around the room at the family pictures on the wall, the fan turning back and forth on the table, the picture of Jesus over the doorway. I don't know what Grace actually saw, but she continued as if she knew she had to get to the end now.

"I ran and hid behind the Holmes house to catch my breath. I looked for Noah at the water tower and called out for him. Then I walked out toward his house, but I still didn't see him. I took my time staying in people's yards and trying to not make a ruckus. Finally I decided to hike back up to the pool to see if he had doubled back there to meet me.

"The nearer I got to the pool, the more my chest seemed to fill up with too much air. So I ran the last few blocks. I heard the clock strike one time. I didn't know exactly what time that meant, though. When I reached the fence by the baby pool, I hollered for Noah two or three times. But he never answered. Something moved behind the office building. I thought, 'Well, if somebody's there, they better come on out and get me.'"

She crossed her arms. None of us adults moved. We knew the ending of this story, but we had to let her get there on her own.

"When I started up the stairs by the deep end of the pool, I saw Noah's shoes lying in the grass. I thought he was trying to hide and scare me."

She put her hand in front of her. "The gate swung back when I pushed it. Then I tiptoed over by the low diving board and looked in the water. His white shirt was shining in the moonlight. He was floating face down, and I thought he was going to pull his head up and roll over and laugh at me."

She hung her head, then rubbed her hand across her forehead like an old woman.

"But he didn't. He stayed with his face in the water not moving at all. I knew then something was bad wrong. I think I may have laid down on the concrete. I remember the heat from the concrete against my face made it hard to breathe. I felt awful."

Grace stood there in the middle of the floor. I looked at the lawyers with their grim faces. Mother Rachel had tears streaming down her face. Preacher Doaks stared out the window. Then Grace's thin shoulders shook, and she looked at me.

"Then I got up and ran. I went and got Meshac, and she went back up to the pool with me. That's all I really remember about that night."

Grace was glassy-eyed when she finished. No one knew what to do next. Edna pushed herself up from the couch and placed Grace's purse on her little arm. She bent down low and whispered something in Grace's ear as she pushed her out the door. One of the men took her a glass of water on the porch. I could see the top of her head through the window as she stood and waited for the grownups to follow. We were all quiet on the drive back.

That summer marked a change in a lot of ways. After the drowning, they drained the pool and refilled it. It took nearly two weeks before the water warmed up enough to swim. Grace spent whole days at the playground or creeping around spying on people. Her bare feet were hard as nails, and I caught her more than once walking on those pin-sharp gravel bits on the side of the road—just to see if it would hurt.

After long days of moping and crying in secret and even longer nights of not sleeping, we finally began to ease out of the numbness. Even though it was a horrible summer in Nuanz, Tennessee, it was still summer. People settled in and slowed down. We didn't talk about it so much. Maybe it would all go away. But we knew it would never be the same. I learned that the hard way, as did Grace. We all did.

PART III
AUTUMN EQUINOX
SEPTEMBER 23, 1960

What's Fair Is Fair

Dayton County had the longest-running fair in Tennessee. Every September for one hundred years, the fair had opened in Nuanz the next-to-last week of September. It was near the fall equinox, when days and nights were of equal length. This year the people in Nuanz craved a balance in their lives. Things were all out of whack.

Beginning in August, country people prepared for their county fair. The first night was livestock judging, from pigs to cattle to sheep. There were tractor displays, information booths, and the women's pavilion filled with flowers, preserves, and homemade biscuits. Women all over the county vied for the most perfect marigold or the best quilt.

The carnival was another world to itself. The carnies came in the

Saturday before and began setting up the midway. There were traditional rides like the merry-go-round, the Ferris wheel, and the bumper cars. Then there would be the ride that none of us had ever seen before—the Tarantula or the Planet Jumper. Hawkers hollered at you—"Hey, little lady, pick up five ducks for fifty cents, win yourself a prize."

Testosterone oozed from the pores of the pistol-fast baseball pitchers knocking over bottles to win some girl's heart. Feats of strength, daring deeds, and freaks of nature were all there for the asking. It became more than a game of chance. You took risks at the fair—from riding the scary ride to seeing the two-headed pig. This was when you tried something different or you went home wishing you had. Cotton candy, candied apples, pronto pups, and fiddlesticks called to be consumed. The Crazy House, the Ghost Ride, the bearded lady, and the fortune-tellers drew the really big crowds. The best was after ten o'clock when the hoochie-coochie dancers came out on the stage. The guys dug into their jeans pockets for lots of one-dollar bills. It was initiation time into the mysterious world of strippers and female bodies.

So the fair was coming to town, and everybody talked about it the week before. I remembered the fair at home. It was in Stantonville, the county seat. We never went much when we were little, but as teenagers we'd hitch a ride over to the carnival on the weekends. Lots of kids would get kind of goofy at the carnival. The bright lights and rides and food were great fun. As they got older, couples would pair off for the ride through the Tunnel of Love, or you'd go after a certain boy in your bumper car.

I never had a real boyfriend. There were a couple of guys in school that I liked, but never in a carnal way. I was more like one of the boys. We might pretend we were a couple, but both of us knew we weren't serious. So when this guy looked at me at the corn dog stand on Monday's free gate night, I really didn't think too much of it. It was kind of the flirty, fair thing going on, but it was nice.

He probably thought I was somebody else, I said to myself.

When I didn't give him the eye back, he drifted off and I thought that was the end of him. But I saw him again on Saturday night.

Jerry Lee Lewis was performing at the fair that night. The Jerry Lee Lewis. I had heard his record, *Great Balls of Fire*, and he was making all the county fairs in Tennessee to help his record sales. He was supposed to really be able to tear up a piano. Edna and I were going to go after the cafe closed on Saturday night. Grace wanted me to take her, but I told her she should be home studying her Sunday school lesson. That was kind of cruel, I know, but she's come to expect such from me.

Edna came by a little after eight, and I changed out of my uniform in the back of the cafe. I forgot to bring my regular shoes, so I had on my clunky waitress shoes. We were milling about on the carnival side, looking at ourselves in the crazy house mirrors and laughing like twelve-year-olds, when I saw this guy again. The same one I had seen on Monday night. It took me a minute to place him, and then I looked away before he actually caught me looking at him.

Edna knew everybody and their uncle. As we walked through the rides and concession stands, people hollered at her. She was like a queen with her subjects.

"Hidey, Melvin. How're you and the missus tonight?"

Not one note of sarcasm lay underneath that comment. Mrs. Melvin seemed as happy to see Edna as Mr. Melvin. The single guys were a little more brazen.

"Hey, Edna. Come over here."

"I ain't got time to fool with you tonight."

"Oh, please. Just a minute."

She kept right on walking. Edna's one of those women that you don't necessarily want to grow up to be, but you sure do value as a friend. She was coy when she needed to be, but when you needed bald-faced lying, she could handle that, too. She ran the town in one sense, and everybody, including the mayor, knew it.

Her mama's family had lived around Nuanz for several generations, and they had owned a lot of land. Misfortune followed, though, and her mama married beneath herself. Illegal liquor and cheap rental property got them through the lean years. Her granddad began with homemade moonshine and wine. Then her dad and uncles picked up the trade with bootleg whiskey. Even after package stores opened over the Tennessee line, her dad and uncles were the ones who could sell you a pint of whiskey past midnight on Saturday, and there'd be no questions asked.

The backroom operations at a couple of their houses gave Edna enough to hold over most everybody's head as long as she lived. She didn't abuse it, though. She knew how to use it and when and, lucky for us all, she kept Nuanz from going under a few times when times were bad.

There were some kids standing by the duck pond booth. The young boy working the booth looked bored as he watched the kids pick up the plastic ducks from the water.

"What's your number on the bottom there?"

The little girl held it up for him to see. "Oh, you got a three, five, and nine. Let's see what you might get."

"Have you ever been married, Edna?" I asked her as we strolled along.

"Lord, no, child. Why would I want a husband to keep up with? I got plenty of problems with my regular guys bothering me all the time." We stopped and looked toward the dart-throwing booth.

"Thank God I've never had to worry about where I was going to live or what I was going to eat. My daddy saw to that. My mama taught me a lot about people."

We walked on to the dart-throwing booth. "For some reason, I was born with enough sense to listen to my mama most of the time. I didn't have to learn everything by trial and error."

She leaned over and picked up one of the darts. The lady behind the counter said, "Five throws for a dollar."

Edna nodded her head and laid down a dollar bill. She felt the weight of the dart and looked over at the balloons on the wall. "You know, Meshac . . ." She threw the first dart and hit the wall. "That way of learning can cost you." Her second and third darts missed the balloons.

She aimed carefully with her tongue in the corner of her mouth. "You got marrying . . ." The dart hit the blue balloon and she grinned.

"Last one." The dart nicked the red one.

The lady handed Edna a plastic coin purse and a comb. "Want to try again?"

Edna shook her head and we started off. "So are you?"

"What? Marrying? Oh, God, no."

By then we were at the grandstand, and people were climbing up into the seats getting ready for the show. The stage was a flatbed trailer on the baseball field situated about halfway between home plate and the pitcher's mound. Extra portable lights were set up, and black cords snaked their way down the trailer to the dugout where young men huddled with headsets. The outfield was lit up, and the scoreboard still had the results of the last Babe Ruth game—Home 5, Visitors 1. We found space about halfway up, and the lights went out as we sat down.

The wooden bleachers were old and hard, but I didn't feel a thing for the next hour and a half. The spotlight came on, and a young, blond man appeared on the stage. Dressed in a shiny coat and black trousers, he acted nervous until he sat down on the piano bench and played two songs straight out. The crowd went crazy. We stomped our feet and clapped our hands until they throbbed. He coaxed and begged us until he had us eating out of his hand. Halfway through, he leaned over to the mike and said, "I'd give a hundred dollars for a cold drink." That's when Tater Head Carson jumped over the right-field fence and ran to the stage with a cup. Jerry Lee wouldn't reach over to get it, though. I think it scared him. The men grabbed Tater Head and carried him out the front gate.

"I love you, man," he bellowed, and the crowd roared along with him.

Jerry Lee gave a double take. "I better watch what I say."

Edna poked me with her elbow. "See that man over there?" She pointed out to the edge of the fence. "That's Cleveland White, the local commander of the National Guard." A stocky man in uniform stood over in the left outfield.

"Cleve said Jerry Lee was out at the Elks Club late after hours." Edna leaned over toward me. "Some of the regulars were shooting craps in the back room, and Jerry Lee and his band came by looking for a beer. Most of the guys didn't even know who he was, but Jackie, the bartender, told Cleve, 'This man out here says he's that singer Jerry Lee Lewis, and he wants us to sell him a couple of beers.' Cleve walked over and looked out the side window. Sure enough, it looked like Jerry Lee.

"'Hell, let him in,' he told them."

Edna checked to see if anybody was hanging onto her every word. "Sure enough, it was Jerry Lee and three of his band members. They all sat there together until about four this morning, and Cleve and them hatched up this idea."

She paused and lowered her voice. "They're gonna set off one of those detonators from the armory. Cleve told me so we'd be prepared, but everybody in town knows it already."

Lewis sang song after song—"Crazy Arms," "Whole Lotta Shakin' Goin' On," "Breathless." He had been on stage over an hour and a half, and we knew he was getting near the end. He had thrown his coat off a long time ago. His white shirt was unbuttoned to his waist and clung to his thin body. The perspiration poured off him. His hair was a halo of golden curls.

He still hadn't sung "Great Balls of Fire." We were afraid he was going to skip it. Some of the crowd starting chanting, "Great balls of fire, great balls of fi-re." It finally dawned on the band what they were saying. Jerry Lee covered the mike and said something to the band. They all laughed. Jerry Lee said to the crowd, "I was getting to it, just taking my time."

We laughed as if we were one giggly teenager. Then we waited. Cleve stood up against the fence, his Guard cap pushed to the back of his head. Jerry Lee cleared his throat and took the microphone off its stand. He looked across the baseball diamond into the left outfield and shaded his eyes with his hand. His voice was an intimate, low rumble, but we heard every word: "Now don't you guys do anything crazy out there."

That got an even bigger laugh. He looked back at us and grinned. Then he replaced the mike and bent it even lower over the piano. He sat down and started the song. I've never seen anybody play a piano like that. His fingers pumped up and down like the needle on a sewing machine—sharp and relentless. They moved so fast they were a blur. The sweat poured off his body, and he slung it off with his gyrations. He played with his feet, his butt, his elbows, and his hands. He had been going hard and fast, and suddenly he stood up and knocked the piano bench back onto the floor.

Cleve dropped his hand, and the guys released one of the Guard's A number 1 detonators. The boom shook the seats and electrified the very air. Jerry Lee Lewis held his hands up and said, "God damn—whoo!" My ears popped, and we all held our breath as we swallowed the six words we knew by heart. Then everybody was hollering and screaming and jumping up and down. The band hustled off the stage and wouldn't come back even when we kept clapping for ten minutes.

After the concert, we kept sitting and talking. Nobody wanted to leave. It was a good fall night, and as the lights went out, you could see the stars above.

Finally we walked out the gate, and I saw the same guy again leaning up against a light pole. I guess I was braver then as I looked at him and he said, "Hey there." I mumbled something and then ducked my head like a kid. Edna never quit talking as if none of that registered with her at all. She dropped me off at the motel a little after midnight, and I pulled on my warm T-shirt and sweatpants and sat outside my room. I didn't want to go in and let the night end yet.

Leaning back against the wooden lawn chair, I gazed at the stars. It felt as if I could reach up and touch them. I picked out the constellations I knew—the Little Dipper with the North Star its anchor, The Seven Sisters, Orion's Sword. I remembered sitting on our back stoop at home listening to the owls hoot and looking at the stars. I used to wonder what would happen to me. I had big plans like anybody, but there was loneliness inside me that I couldn't quite get over. And now here I was in Nuanz sitting and looking at the same stars. I was a different person, but the stars were the same.

I did the worst thing any human can do. I took a man's life. It wasn't an accident. I planned it and prepared for it. I don't know if George hadn't said what he did or come after me there in the field if I would have shot him anyway. I think I would have. That was my intent. The guilt and remorse are just not there. I don't want to be caught. But who does? Just because I think the world is better off without George doesn't excuse what I did. I know that. But I think I can live better with his death than I could live with what he was about to do to Irene. I couldn't bear for anybody else to go through that. Will God forgive me? If there is a God, then why did He let George rape me? Answer that.

So knowing this about me, it's a wonder I could ever love anybody at all. But here in Nuanz I felt pretty safe. I felt like maybe I could make up to the world for what I did. Maybe that's why I let Grace hang around and why I put up with some stuff. I know there's nobody out there to take care of me but me. Meshac, what's done is done. As Mama used to say, there's no need to cry over spilt milk.

Then, as I sat outside the motel, the guy from the fair walked up out of the darkness and said, "Hey" again. I know I looked shocked.

"Where'd you come from?" I blurted out. He shrugged his shoulders.

"I didn't come from anywhere. I'm going to my room."

"Oh."

"They do allow other people to sleep here, don't they?"

I didn't know what to say.

He crossed his arms. "Didn't I see you at the fair tonight?"

"Yeah," was all I could say. He looked even better up close.

"Jerry Lee is pretty good, isn't he?"

"Yeah, I thought he was good." Idiot, I'm a frigging idiot. Then I said, "I hated to end the night after it had been so good."

"I know what you mean," he nodded. "Can I sit down for a minute?"

I don't know where I got the courage, but I said yes. That was pretty much how it started. If Jerry Lee Lewis hadn't come to the Dayton County Fair on that Saturday night, I would have never had the nerve to sit there and talk to this complete stranger half the night. I was afraid the sun was going to come up before we parted. It must have been the music and the stars and the feeling in the air that autumn night that affected me. It was like that bass on the piano had chipped away little icicles of fear that had kept me so cold, and I wanted to talk and talk and talk to this man. I felt that if I didn't, I might not ever connect with any human being again. I didn't want to be that way.

The very idea that some guy would want to talk to me or touch or kiss me was so foreign to me. I guess that's why I didn't pick up on this guy coming on to me. He said he had been in the cafe a few times. He was nice-looking and probably near my (phony) age. But I didn't even see myself as anyone a guy would want to flirt with, much less talk to.

As we were sitting there in those chairs with the moon shining on the pavement and the dew glistening in the grass, I would come back to that thought—if you only knew what I had done. But I kept sitting and talking about whatever popped into my head.

Then all of a sudden the sky began to lighten over in the east, and I knew the stars would begin to fade. Joe (that was his name) stood up and stretched his arms overhead like a tomcat. He placed his hands on the arms of my chair and leaned into my face and said, "I'm gonna kiss you good night now."

I didn't say a word; I closed my eyes and waited. His lips pressed against mine and parted them a little, and I held my breath hoping this kiss would last a long time. The darkness behind my eyelids streaked with green and yellow lights like fireworks, and those words I had swallowed at the concert shot into my head. Goodness . . .

He stood up and hung his thumbs in the back pockets of his jeans. He looked really tall standing there while I swooned in my chair. I couldn't move. He smiled and said something and walked out of the ring of light. I sat back and scrunched my legs up in the chair, hugging my knees with both arms. Please, I thought, let me enjoy this a little bit longer.

The sky stayed still for a few moments. The light was gradually eating up the darkness. My breath slowed, but my heart still ratcheted against my chest all the way into my ears. I closed my eyes and rested my forehead against my knees, thinking, remembering, and floating a little bit longer.

I was stiff when I stood up. I shuffled into my room, threw off my clothes, and climbed between the cool sheets. I didn't think I could sleep, but I drifted off and slept soundly until a car door slamming woke me the next morning.

Tears and Kisses

I lay in bed going over the night before. I couldn't believe that Joe had kissed me. Was it Jerry Lee Lewis, the Tunnel of Love, or plain old lust that made me want him to kiss me? That kiss made me feel like a real human being, not a murderer. Why would Joe even want to kiss me?

George—you son of a bitch. Let go of me. Seems like part of me is sunk in Hale's Swamp wrapped up in that same tarp and weighted down with mud and sand. The carp have nibbled on my toes, I'll admit that, but there's still enough of me left to push off the bottom and swim to the top. He kissed me. Remember that, Meshac. He kissed ME.

It was Sunday, and the cafe was closed. I decided I'd take Grace on a bike ride. I didn't even make it to her house before I ran into her. She came from behind Mrs. Towater's house as if she had been standing there waiting for me.

"Hi," she said. "How was your big night at the fair?"

"Okay. I was on my way to your house."

She looked at me.

"Want to go for a picnic or a ride or something?"

"I dunno."

"We could get some leftovers from the cafe and ride our bikes out in the country. The leaves may be turning."

She looked at me as any kid would when I mentioned the leaves were turning. But I could tell she wanted to go for a ride.

"Come on," I begged. Just to make her feel good. "It'll be fun."

"Okay, but I'll have to ask Aunt Virginia. She's bugging me to death nowadays wanting to know where I am all the time."

"She's concerned."

"Naw, she's nosy."

"Go tell Aunt Virginia. I'll pick up some food and meet you on Court Square."

"Want me to bring us something to drink?"

"That'd be great." I turned back toward downtown to see what I could find at the cafe.

Once we got on the road, the sun came out even brighter and warmed our shoulders and bent heads. It felt good to be out in the light with the breeze from bicycling cooling my face. I gave out before she did, of course, and had to stop for water. I tilted my head back as the ice cubes in the jar ran down and hit my nose.

"Where do you want to go?"

Grace didn't hesitate for a second.

"There's this secret place Noah and me used to go when we played out here. It's down this road by the Pinkerton place. There used to be a house up on the hill and it's got a creek with a waterfall."

"Lead on, O Queen Eternal," I said. She actually laughed and jumped onto her bike. I followed close enough to keep her in sight. Her legs pumped up and down and her head stuck out from her body like a chicken loose on the prowl for a fat worm. I lost sight of her for a minute. When I cleared the hill, I couldn't see her bike anywhere, and I caught my breath. Then I saw a flash behind a stand of sumac, and she reappeared at the top of the old Pinkerton place. She was right. There was a stand of maple trees there that must have surrounded a house at one time. I got off and pushed my bike through the overgrown front yard. Grace was squatting on a square of concrete that used to be the front stoop. She picked up a piece of jagged rock and was scratching over the blackened stone.

"Whew, that was a pretty fast ride."

She said nothing.

"Listen, Grace, I know you may not want to talk about it, but I miss Noah, too. And it's okay."

She didn't lift her head. Her lank, blond hair covered both sides of her face. We stayed that way for a minute: her head bent, scraping the rock, me looking at the top of her head and her scrawny little body. Then her head started shaking, and I thought she might be laughing, but the most horrible sound came out of her. I reached down to grab her, and she knocked me over. She started kicking and flailing her arms and screaming. Her face was white and scrunched up like an old woman. Tears flooded her face. When I could get her to stop moving, she went limp, but the tears kept pouring. She didn't say a word.

We sat there a long time. I don't know when the tears for Noah ended and the tears for Grace and Meshac began. Maybe they were all mixed up together. I felt hollowed out inside all the way to the soles of my feet. There was nothing there.

I had never felt so alone and hopeless as I did right then. When I cried, the weight of all those years of shame, hurt, and aloneness came out. I cried for that skinny little black boy who had only the love of his grandmother and a sassy little white girl to fill him with some degree of happiness. And I cried for Gracie, who had no little girls to giggle with or a warm young mother to tuck her into bed at night with wisps of Cashmere Bouquet wafting her off to sleep. It was as if everything I had pushed back down inside me—from George to no money, no daddy, no mama who cared about anything, to no brightness for most of my life—it came out of that hollowness like a swoosh from an evil bird of prey.

Then when I was all cried out and the tears dried on my face, Grace got the hiccups. We sat there and looked at each other. I patted her on the head and said, "Everyone needs a good cry every once in a while." To myself, a damn long cry. Here I had not been kissed since I was thirteen years old on Margie Sandiver's hayride by David Talbot. Now within twenty-four hours I had been kissed under the moonlight by a complete stranger, swooned like a sick puppy, and cried my eyes red with a ten-year-old girl. Geez—heart work is holy ground. Holier than I am used to. How can a sinner like me know anything about holy ground?

I lay there, vaguely aware that Grace was beside me. What was the use? Why should I even open my eyes, sit up, or take another breath? Why? But I opened my eyes, and the blueness of the sky hurt me and made a pain run across my forehead like a streak of fire, but I kept my eyes open. Then a yellow leaf from the maple tree blew into my sight, and it floated up and then down, flipped itself over two or three times, drifted out of my sight, and then softly floated up again. The wind played with that one single leaf, and I watched and did not think one single thought.

When I sat up, it seemed as if something was different. The light was whiter. The breeze picked my hair off my forehead, and I realized I was sweating. Then as my vision cleared even more, all of these yellow, red, and orange maple leaves began swirling and twirling above us. As if they were saying, "Look at all of us. There's thousands of us flying and falling and flying again."

I didn't know what to say to Grace. At first I thought I wouldn't say anything, but then I thought of my own silence-filled childhood.

"Are you okay?"

"I dunno. Feel kind of weird. I guess I kind of lost it."

"No, Grace, maybe you found it. Sometimes it's good to cry and scream rather than keep stuff inside."

"I'll never see him again."

"I know. You'll always miss him, but the hole inside will begin to close up. I promise."

"Why did somebody hurt Noah like that?"

She let me put my arm around her. I grabbed the rock and started writing her name as I tried to explain the unexplainable:

"There are so many things we don't understand, Gracie. We can hope somebody figures out things someday. People do things they shouldn't. People get hurt. People die. Sometimes that makes you want to hurt somebody, too. But what would that prove? When would it end?"

I clamped my mouth shut. Enough of that, old girl, I thought. We sat there another minute.

"So you said there was a waterfall up here?"

Grace took me to a ditch on the back of the property. The bank was steep, but we climbed down and walked beside the creek. There was a little waterfall up ahead, probably a three-foot drop, and the sound of the falling water was nice. We walked back and forth over the mossy rocks in the creek.

"Noah and me used to come here and wade in the creek."

I didn't say anything.

"We'd catch tadpoles with our hands and throw them on each other."

She bent over and splashed water at me. I didn't mind. We wandered back toward our bikes, and there on the west side was a row of red flowers.

"Look, Grace, red spider lilies. I remember them from home."

She knelt and picked one of them and tucked it inside her shirt. The pollen made a streak down her neck, and I could see the tips of the flower bouncing as she walked.

"Someone's mother must have planted these here a long time ago. Promise me you won't tell where we found them," she said.

I pledged with an X over my heart and spat through my fingers. That made her laugh. Picking a lily, I stuck it in my hair. We ate the leftover chicken and drank the last of the water, then started back to town.

I looked for Joe for a whole week. I found myself looking for him at the cafe. After I finished work in the evenings, I sat outside thinking I might see him. Finally one afternoon I got up enough nerve to ask Loretta what had become of him. She cut her eyes at me. "What do you want to know for?"

I felt myself blush. "I don't know. I haven't seen him since the night of the fair."

She shook her head. "Well, not that it's any of our business, but he works on the riverboat out of Danville. He's out for six weeks and then back for two and gone again. Least that's how it's been the last year. He used to rent a house here, but now we keep a room ready for him when he's coming back in. Want to see when he's due back?"

"Oh, no. I don't care. I was just wondering."

"Uh-huh," she mumbled.

I buried my head in my library book and didn't look up till I heard her shoes scraping against the concrete walk. Then I tucked that night away into the empty place inside of me. I didn't ponder it but let it ride there real easy-like.

Fall gradually let go of us. The nights began to get cooler, and then a warm day would reappear and you would think, "Well, it's not over yet." The sumac lost its leaves and left those deep magenta pods pointing upward. Flocks of birds came into town at sundown. The days were gray more than blue. Hawks hung out alone in the sky. My bones told me that winter was coming. The planets rolled over, and the constellations shifted into their new places above our heads.

I decided to call home. When I heard Aunt Flora's voice, it cut through my midsection like a knife. I hung up. Sweet Aunt Flora, who took better care of us than our own mother.

The next day, Irene answered when I tried again. I sat there when I heard her voice. She was about to hang up when I said, "Irene, it's me."

"Meshac?"

"Yeah."

"God, where are you?"

"I can't say right now. How's Mama?"

"'Bout dead."

"Is she still at home?"

"Naw, she's been in the ward at the hospital about a month now. George has disappeared."

"He has?"

"Yeah, nobody knows what happened to him, and Mama wouldn't get out of bed after that. I think she's lost her mind."

"Did George leave town?"

"They found our car over in Stantonville, but the tires was flat. They think he may have gotten on a bus and taken off. Are you still in Florida?"

"How'd you know I was in Florida?"

"Katy said you'd been talking about taking off. I think she's mad you didn't tell her first, though."

"Well, I'm not there anymore."

Her voice trembled a little. "Well, when are you coming home?"

"I dunno, Irene." I tried not to picture that look on her face that I've seen before.

"Is something the matter?"

"No, I'm trying to get out of Wicket."

She sat there a moment. "Looks like you've done that all right."

"You going to school?"

"Yeah, but I hate it."

"You and Roy staying with Aunt Flora?"

"Yep. That at least is good."

"Sure it is."

"Do you wanna talk to her?"

"Not right now. I gotta go, but I'll try and call back in a few weeks."

"Are you sure you're okay?"

"Yes, Irene. I'm fine. See ya."

I felt glad I had talked to Irene. I hated that Mama was in the hospital, but even if I was there, there's nothing I could have done. My stomach had a heavy rock right in the middle of my gut. After I walked out into the street and headed toward the cafe, I started feeling better. Several of my customers spoke to me as I walked down the street. Mrs. Thornton waved at me through the drugstore window. I liked Nuanz.

October brought a balance of warm days and cool nights. Crops were coming in, and footballs were flying on Friday nights at the local high schools. Overall, there was this pervading sense of reaping what we had sown. Things had quieted down with the sit-ins in Jackson and the murder investigation in Nuanz.

I had forgotten that it was trick-or-treat night. Somebody mentioned at the cafe about having plenty of candy on hand. Surely no one would come to the Nuanz Motor Inn to trick or treat. Unless it was Grace.

I couldn't imagine her dressing up as a ghost or even a hobo. But sure enough, there was a faint knock on my door at eight thirty, and I flung it open, expecting Grace or some goblin at least. I nearly fainted when I saw Joe standing there with a paper sack.

"Trick or treat?" He grinned and so did I.

"Uh. You've caught me without any treats, guess you'll have to do the tricking."

"What do you think the sheriff will think about me soaping up his windows?"

"I don't know that'd go over too well."

I looked outside. It was dark and a little cool. "Wanna come in?"

"Sure." He stepped in quickly as if I might change my mind.

He turned the one straight chair around and straddled it with his hands resting easily over the back. He still held his paper sack. I could feel myself grinning a goofy grin.

"Got anything in there?"

He handed it over. I looked inside and spied my favorite candy bar, Goo Goo Cluster, resting on top of a paperback book. I was intrigued, of course.

"I'll take the Goo Goo. Whose book is that?"

"Yours if you want it."

I held it up to see the title. *The Incredible Journey.*

I should have felt uneasy in my room alone with a man, but I didn't. I sat on the foot of my bed and leaned back on my hands. Oops, shouldn't have done that. I straightened up and made sure my feet stayed on the floor. Joe looked around my room and leaned over as he inspected my three books on the table.

"What's this one—*Celestial Signs?*"

"That's my bible from my . . ."

"Oh, yeah, your auntie who taught you that stargazing superstitious stuff."

I laughed. "That's close. Tell me about your boat trip."

His eyes lit up. "How'd you know I been on a boat?"

"Oh, I have my ways."

It got easier to talk to him. After a while, he stood up to leave. I even allowed his hand to touch my back as we stood at the door when he said good night.

So what was I going to do if he wanted to kiss me again? Should I say yes or no or wait?

Then Grace jumped out of the darkness at us with a loud boo. We sprang apart as if we were guilty of something. She didn't even pretend to stop and ask for a treat. Guess she had accomplished what she set out to do. Joe shrugged and walked around the corner. I was glad for the small interruption.

Mr. Davis taught us in General Science class that the tilt of the earth was calculated at 23 degrees and 27 minutes. That slight tilt on its axis creates the seasons as we spin around the sun. Equinoxes. Solstices. Sometimes one small thing can tilt your own world over—like those bobbing ducks at the county fair or a light touch on a girl's arm. I know I am tilted. Is there any hope I could tilt back the other way?

What's Love Got to Do with It?

I had never met anyone like Edna Love in my life. Edna was a mover and shaker. The things she shook up were not always what you would expect. She could make the head teller at the Bank of Commerce get weak in the knees passing her on the sidewalk. A noisy room of adult conversation could stop on her regal entrance. It was hard to explain Edna's effect on people. She could fool you; she was wily and secretive.

Edna was a short woman, little wide of the beam, with dyed black hair that she wore in an upswept French twist hairdo. Her face was always made up—a tad heavy-handed. Her clothes lent her that tramp look—low-cut blouses, short skirts, and tight pants. She wore dangling earrings with lots of bracelets and glitter. Nearly every finger had a ring, and she liked to stick shiny, enameled chopsticks into the top of her coiffure. She called everybody "Hon," from the police chief to the town drunk.

I had learned a lot about her these past few months. Edna was a single woman. She had never been alone, though. Growing up, she had an attentive mother and father. Her father's reputation was questionable, but her mother's background gave it a little credence. Her ancestors may be far removed, but even now if you owned some land in Nuanz you had something. Nobody could take that away from you. No matter what succeeding generations had or had not done, you still had that same blood running in your veins. You owned it. That gave you an edge in your confidence if you could keep up your courage. Edna was good at that.

She had never been married, but she was engaged once many years ago to a guy. He left under dire circumstances. No one ever heard from him again. Edna's mother had the pedigree, but it was her daddy's side of the family that had the ready cash. Taking advantage of man's naturally sinful side, the Loves began with homemade wine and continued with whatever else was needed.

From the 1920s up till the late '40s, her father's bootlegging provided enough money to live fairly well, buy up some cheap rental property, and dabble in several businesses. Edna was the only child and grew up in the middle of her daddy's business. Packages were sold out the back door in certain sections of town, and the law looked the other way for some very lucrative reasons. Edna finished ninth grade and—face it—made her living on her back for twenty years. But she was smart about her money, and in the last few years she had become more of an entrepreneur and manipulator than the town's loose woman. Her family's name and heritage gave her a degree of respectability that could only be understood if you lived there.

Edna usually had two or three steady boyfriends who acted as if they didn't know the others existed. More and more, she was accepted on a certain level by the city fathers, and her business head was actually respected. The surprise was that she was a relatively rich woman, and she helped a lot of people in Nuanz in different ways. Edna could tell a good tale, too. This often made her the center of attention wherever a group gathered. She liked that—being the center of attention.

I was the opposite. I had never thought of myself as pretty. As a girl, I felt most comfortable in my blue jeans and T-shirts walking in the fields or climbing trees. George ruined my childhood that spring, and I never could get back to that easy way of being again. All I wanted was to disappear in the hope that no one would notice me at all. That is, until I started taking control of my life.

My daddy had an old .45 Colt pistol. I had found it in the shed beside the barn when I was fourteen years old. It was wrapped up in an oily rag and an old flannel shirt of his and was at the bottom of a tow sack under the loose floorboards of the shed. I was fascinated with it. Amazed at how heavy and cold it felt in my hands, I would check on it every week or so. My hands would test the weight of it. I would heft it from one hand to another. I pointed it at the side of the barn and posed with it like Roy Rogers. It made me feel better knowing it was out there, wrapped in my daddy's shirt, waiting. It helped me to sleep at night, and it was always there in the back of my mind like the golden grail. It was the hidden treasure, and I was the only one who knew it was there.

When I got my first job, I bought some bullets for it. The guy at Burnett's Hardware in town kind of felt sorry for me, I think, and he never squawked any about selling me the bullets. The first time he said, "What are you wanting this for?" and I said, "To shoot in a gun." He never bothered me again.

I target practiced for two years, nearly every Saturday. I would make up different places I would say I was going. Sometimes I would say I was going to Katy's house. Sometimes I would say I was going walking, or looking for blackberries, or picking up pecans down in the field. Most of the time nobody said anything, and it got to be easier and easier to slip away. I practiced as much as I could. At first, the idea of killing George was a vague possibility—way out there maybe in the future. It felt like the whisper of a forgotten conversation, fading for a while and then suddenly right there in my face.

Was it highly unlikely then that Edna and I would become fast friends? Was that why I ended up in Nuanz? Did the stars guide me here? When I stopped in Love's Launderette that day, did I sense more would be washed away than the grime of my journey?

Love's Launderette had done more cleansing than the First Baptist Church would ever do. There were no judgments amid the pink washers and the aqua "hottest dryers in town." All your dirty laundry came out as good as new after a trip to Edna's launderette. There was something reassuring and nice about the shiny concrete floors, the smell of soap and bleach, and that sanitizing hot air. The windows frosted over in the winter, and the doors stayed open in the summer. The customers had a purpose, a reason to be there. Sort the dirty, soiled work clothes of their husbands and the stained, grimy play clothes of their children; then fill the washers; pour in the blue detergents, white crystal grains of bleach, and pink, fragrant softener. The quarters fit the slots and easily slid into the silver box; voila, the lid went down, and the water poured in. Then we sat and thought our own thoughts, visited with others, and watched a toddler in his last pair of clean diapers wobble up and down the row of washers. After we pulled the clothes from the dryer and folded and pressed out the wrinkles, we felt like we had done something, at least. Sometimes doing laundry can save a soul more than fifteen minutes of hellfire preaching could ever do.

Stopping at Love's Launderette that first day, I had no idea that would be the way to come clean again. Edna knew everything that went on in Nuanz, and by the time I walked into Pierce's Pool Room, she knew I was alone and needed help. Ah, Edna was good at that—taking in strays and working things out. That's why the sheriff knew to take Edna with him when he went to Mother Rachel's. Edna was behind the scenes and in front of them, too—directing, prodding, pushing, and moving people and things around. She made the world work for her and those she cared about. If those decorated chopsticks could talk, what they must have seen and heard.

As fall slid nearer to winter, I could tell Edna was different.

"I hate winter," Edna said one day over coffee in the cafe. "I don't know if my blood is thin or what, but I dread winter more every year."

I just nodded my head as I sipped my own coffee.

"I'm bored out of my gourd. I feel like roaming around today like some old tomcat and pouncing on somebody."

"Well, I hope it's not me. I don't need any pouncing, thank you." The cafe was empty after the morning rush.

"Come on, kid. Let's go for a ride and see what we can get into."

I told Rob I was taking my break, hung up my apron, and followed Edna. We climbed into her Caddy and started cruising, for what or whom I didn't know yet.

I looked at Edna sideways as we rolled down the street. I had learned a lot from Edna these past few months. God love her, she wasn't a deep thinker, but she had enough sense to know that many times the gut was a better indicator than the head. Certainly don't ever trust the heart. It could fool you and get you into the worst kind of trouble. That's why Edna liked working on desires. She explained it to me one night over a glass of sherry while leaning over the counter at her Oasis Club.

"Desires, Meshac. You know, physical needs like hunger and sex and food on the table, or no-no's like revenge, jealousy, vanity, and lust. Some things we can control; some we think we can. But you don't know for sure till you try."

I remember she wagged her finger at me and then nodded her head as if to convince both of us she knew what she was talking about. Edna knew when the time was right for something and went ahead and did it. She and I were kind of alike in that way.

She circled the square again and then headed down College Street. "I believe it's about time for a talk with the sheriff."

Edna had on her purple-flowered, skintight skirt and V-neck sweater with lots of beads and long, sparkly earrings. She patted the sachet of Fleurs de Rocaille between her ample breasts and studied herself in the rearview mirror. Those glittery enameled chopsticks nodded as I heard her say for the umpteenth time—"Edna, you beautiful thing. Don't you ever die."

She looked over at me with her head cocked back and gave me one of those wiseass "don't mess with me" looks that I knew the poor sheriff would be getting soon.

Sure enough, two blocks down the road we saw Sheriff Hensley pulled over in his squad car, sipping his coffee. Poor man, I nearly felt sorry for him.

Edna pulled up and waved her arm at him. He climbed out of the car and sauntered over with his steaming coffee cup. I shrank down, hoping he wouldn't notice me but knowing he couldn't help but see me.

"Hello, Edna. Howdy, Meshac."

I nodded my head.

"How you doing, hon?" purred Edna.

"Well, can't you tell, I'm about as busy as a one-legged man in an ass-kicking contest. How 'bout you?"

Edna laughed that deep, infectious laugh. "I thought I'd pay you a little visit."

"Will here do as well?"

She smiled up at Sheriff Hensley, and for a moment they both looked like they really enjoyed being in each other's presence. Willard set the coffee cup on the hood of the car and leaned in her window.

"What can I do for you, Edna?"

She paused just long enough. Her eyes were the eyes of a young flirt. If she had a fan, it would have hidden everything but those eyes and what they were saying.

"I don't see you much anymore, Willard."

"I know," he said. "I'm getting too old to hold my own with the likes of you."

"Oh, let's don't talk about getting old. I'd rather talk about the good old days."

They both laughed and bobbed their heads in agreement.

"What do you need today, Edna?"

She glanced my way, then said, "There's four or five things we need to talk about."

"Four or five—how long is this going to take?"

"We can discuss it after hours if you like."

"No, go ahead, but I ain't got all day, you know."

"First, who opened the new bar down on Third Street?"

"Guy named Ron Yarbrough."

"Is he from here?"

"Some kin to the Yarbroughs east of town but not directly, no."

"Is he on the up and up?"

"Yep, so my night shift say."

"Some of my customers claim they can go over there after we close and have another hour or so of drinking."

"I doubt that. Who do you believe, your drunks or me?"

"I wanted to be sure we were all closing at the same hour."

"I'll check it out myself tonight. What else?"

"My girls say they've had some trouble with the Hamilton boys."

"Which ones?"

"Ralph's two youngest ones."

"You sure?"

"Yep. A little too rough and not leaving when their time is up."

"Okay. I'll send Donnie around to talk to them and let Ralph know he might ought to rein them in a bit."

"Thanks." There was a slight pause to indicate a subtle change in the conversation. Edna placed her hands on the steering wheel.

"Met the new Baptist preacher yet?"

The sheriff had to smile over that one.

"Not exactly."

"He sure is holding on a while on those Sunday morning services. Getting everybody awfully stirred up about whiskey, dancing, and hell."

"Well, that's what they're supposed to do, isn't it?"

"Sure, but usually after two or three months they settle back down. He's still going strong, and it's been over six months."

"You know I can't do nothing about that, Edna."

She laughed. "I know. Just wanted to know if you knew him personally. Thought maybe you might introduce us."

"Edna, I fish with the Presbyterian preacher and go pheasant hunting with the Episcopalians. I can't work in the Baptists, too."

They both chortled to themselves, and for a moment there was an ease between the two that let you know they were old friends. Then Edna asked the question she really had on her mind.

"Speaking of preachers, what's that black preacher doing? Brother Doaks, I think?"

The sheriff rocked back on his heels and reached for his coffee. Now they were getting down to it. He took a sip and then leaned in the window again as he answered her.

"About the same, I reckon. Why?"

"Just curious. I hadn't heard anything lately about Noah, and I knew

Preacher Doaks was heading things up locally for those black lawyers up north."

"Well, Edna, you know I can't tell you about certain investigations." He paused and looked at Edna and then me. I turned and studied my door handle intensely. Edna waited for a reply.

"But we are making some progress." He shoved his hat back a little farther and brought the paper cup to his mouth again.

"What does that mean—some?"

"It means what it means, Edna."

"You know I'm not going to say anything. Who do I have to say it to anyway?"

"Let's say we are continuing to follow leads."

"What about the lead of the fight down at Rem's a few days before?"

The sheriff threw his cold coffee on the ground to stall for a moment. "What's that?"

"You know as well as I do about that to-do with the black guy and the white woman. Everybody knows those kids saw something from underneath that bush."

"Everybody?" He looked like he was getting tired of this.

"Did you ever find out what that was about?"

"We're working on it, Edna." Their eyes locked and then the air changed a bit.

"If I know something more, who should I talk to?"

"Me, I guess."

"So now?"

He crossed his arms. All I could see was his belt buckle. Then he leaned down and took off his hat. "How long is this going to take?"

Bless his heart. He looked very old and worn then. I looked away, but I felt sorry for him.

"Well, I'm just trying to help." Edna would not let him get away that easily.

The sheriff sighed. "What would I do without you, Edna?" He patted the car door two quick taps and waited.

She reached for the ignition and started the car. "I hope you never have to find out."

She touched the back of her hair as she checked the rearview mirror. "Come by tonight and we'll have a glass of sherry."

She pulled the shift down to drive and touched the accelerator. Not even a backward glance at poor Willard.

"Take me back to work," I whined. I had broken out in a sweat being that close to the sheriff.

"Don't worry, hon. Rob won't say a word."

We had one more stop by Love's Launderette. Edna nosed the Caddy into the last parking place on the side of the building. The place was full of young mothers with their children. Diaper pails reeked of ammonia, and washers pounded out the grime of families' everyday living. Edna nodded her head at her customers, most of whom didn't even look up from their *True Confessions* magazines. I walked a few paces behind, as a lowly attendant to the queen should. Clubby stood in the doorway. She headed straight for him. He always looked guilty as hell when she turned up like this unannounced.

"How's it going, hon?"

He nodded and licked his lips. "Pretty good this morning."

"Any problems?"

"Number twenty-four is still not filling up all the way."

"Have you called Bobby Joe?"

"Yeah, he's digging out somebody's trench this morning. He'll get to us when he can."

"You got the coins bagged up?"

"Not yet. I wasn't expecting you this early."

Edna gave him the look. For a few seconds, she hovered there at the edge. Clubby shrank a little more, and his head disappeared, turtle-like, inside his shirt collar. I nearly felt sorry for the little old man.

"Get on with it and I'll be back right before noon to make the deposit."

He shuffled back and picked up the keys off the desk.

"This here came in the mail today."

He handed Edna an envelope. She tucked it into her purse, and we walked out to her car. When we got into the car, she dug out the letter. There was no return address, only "Edna Love, Love's Launderette" handwritten in a dark scrawl. She ripped it open, skimmed it, and handed it to me. The letter was on lined paper and read: "I need some money. Shut up that Misha or I will. Black and white don't mix."

I handed it back to her. "What's that all about?"

"I don't know, hon. Maybe we've been pushing somebody's buttons."

I hadn't pushed anybody's buttons. "Why am I involved?"

"Well, folks at the cafe like to talk and repeat whatever's said."

"Meaning me?" I glared at her.

She tucked the letter back inside her purse.

I continued. "I haven't said any more than anybody else."

"Seems somebody disagrees with that."

"Take me back to work."

"I'm on my way."

The lunch crowd was noisy and demanding. Everybody had a complaint about something. We were out of salmon croquettes before eleven thirty. We never run out of those. Even meek Miss Aileen Caraway glared at me when I didn't bring her vinegar for the greens.

"I really need that vinegar for my greens, you know."

"Yes, ma'am. Coming right up."

The kitchen was hot, and the dishes were stacked up everywhere. What a day for the substitute dishwasher to be on duty. Louise had to go find him in the alley, lounged against the back wall smoking. Mr. Adams was in a daze.

"I can't believe I didn't cook enough salmon." He stood and looked all around as if a pan of croquettes was hiding somewhere. I decided to leave him alone.

I nearly went over the edge when Mr. Claude McKnight began counting out his change from a Red Man tobacco sack—one quarter at a time. Ordinarily I would have laughed and waited, but every clink of those coins grated on my nerves. Then I had to rake the coins off into my hands and recount as I put them in the cash register. I didn't even want to think about what he might have left for a tip.

By midafternoon we seemed to have gotten our bearings. Louise and I sat in the front booth sorting silverware and rolling napkins. The dishwasher was long gone, and Rob Adams perched on his stool and stared out the front window. The only sounds were an occasional car passing outside and the hum of the coolers. Two men sat at separate tables smoking and drinking coffee. Louise had the late afternoon shift to make up for the half day she took last week to take her mother to the doctor. I was stalling to keep from thinking about the letter and whatever it might mean. Maybe it was time for me to leave Nuanz.

It was dark as I left the cafe and started home. Traffic was light as most everyone was home from work and settling in for supper. I had worn a light sweater to work, and as I got closer to the hotel, the cold settled around my shoulders. The stars were dimmed by the streetlights, but the motel sign pulled me in like a porch light as I neared home.

Then I heard something behind me, and without even thinking I picked up my feet to scurry into my room. About the time I got my key into the lock, somebody grabbed my arms and jerked me backward. I stumbled, and he tried to throw something over my head. I elbowed him hard and smashed the roll of quarters I carried in my right hand against his jaw. I couldn't see his face as I tried to stand up. Then I screamed, and he started running. I shifted the roll of quarters to my left hand and threw them after him. They burst all over the sidewalk, of course, and all I could think was I had to get inside.

Luckily, the door opened easily, and I threw myself against the door and turned the lock in one quick motion. I didn't turn on the light. With my face against the door, gulping for air, I willed myself to move. After what seemed an eternity, I thought I heard a car start. I still couldn't leave the door, and I let my knees give way and crumpled to the floor. I lay there in the dark until the cold from the floor forced me up. In the now well-lit room, I dug out my duffel bag, threw out the wadded clothes, and pulled my gun and box of bullets out. I loaded the gun, then climbed into bed with my clothes on. The gun lay on the pillow beside my left hip. I felt like I never slept all night. The thinking would not stop.

What had I said? Always popping off my mouth. When would I ever learn? Who was I to be making speeches in the Bluebird Cafe about serving the blacks? Should I leave now, or was it too late? Were they after only me, or Edna and Gracie, too? Shit, shit, shit. My rules and good intentions went flying out that door. Ha. What a sniveling little scaredy cat you are, Mesha, with your big old mean gun.

The next morning, with daylight surrounding me, I was filled again with that cold determination I thought I had left behind in Hale's Swamp. I might have to leave here—that's true—but I would be damned if I was going to let some old, dried-up prune of a man scare me off. I would be more guarded with my talk and check out those dark spaces, wherever they were. I came to escape from old dead George. I had learned a thing or two from Edna Love and little Gracie and those sit-in folks over in Jackson. Fear can hop on your shoulders and ride you down real quick. The more you let it win, the harder it is to take the next breath and get back up. I looked at myself in the mirror that morning and repeated, "I will not be afraid. I will not be afraid. I will not be afraid."

Why was my heart so black? We had to find the one who did this and make him pay. For Noah and for Grace and for me. This was my calling. This was my payback. This was my own personal lunch counter kind of thing. Endure, take it, change. I stepped over the silver quarters scattered on the sidewalk on my way to work. I would rather starve than bend down and pick them up, you damn bastard.

PART IV
WINTER SOLSTICE
DECEMBER 21, 1960

The Rescue

As fall gave way to winter, my apprehensions disappeared like gray wisps of smoke. No one was looking for me here. Grace was getting better. The safety net of friends like Edna, Loretta, and Mr. Adams made me feel protected. Joe was around long enough to be interesting, and then he would leave for a few weeks. I slept better, all through the night, than I had since I was twelve years old. The nightmares with old George rising up from Hale's Swamp quit haunting my dreams. But you know when you let your guard down, that's when the whole shebang can whirl off its axis and sling you out into that vast, no-bottom-to-it abyss. I should have known better.

December was never a great time for me. The Christmas lights and the tiny tree in the drugstore window made me sad. I knew I needed to call home, but I couldn't make myself. I did send an envelope of money to Aunt Flora to help with the presents for Irene and Roy.

I began hanging out more at the Oasis after I finished work at the Bluebird. I yearned for more human connections, and there was always somebody I could talk to at Edna's place. Sometimes I sat and listened to Catfish spin his tales or to the jukebox play the same selections.

The Oasis Bar was on First Street not too far from the cafe, but in the opposite direction of the Nuanz Motor Inn. Edna owned it, and Moose Hudson ran it. The regular customers were on their assigned stools by dark thirty, which arrived early in December. I usually got there around eight o'clock if things went okay. The days I drew first shift I was too tired to stay that late. But other days I could hang out there till closing time, and Edna or one of the guys would give me a ride home.

The night of the rescue was on my first three-day weekend in a long time. I had decided to stay until closing. The TV was turned down low, but I could still catch voices and laughter from time to time. Catfish Somers had finished one of his funny stories when a stranger walked through the door. It was around eleven, still early. The regulars at the bar looked up as he stepped into the circle of light from the hanging wagon-wheel chandelier. Jesse, Robert, and Max all turned back to their Pabst, feigning indifference, but Moose, the bartender, and Johnny, the permanent resident customer, leaned forward to take it all in. Catfish and I watched. The guy was white, short, with black, bushy hair slicked back from his face. His arms looked strong, and he was stout in the middle. He walked as if he was at home here in this den of iniquity. As he sat on a stool near the far end and waited for Moose, he looked around the joint as if to check the exits. He ordered a Falstaff in a glass, and Moose reached into the cooler for the heavy, frosted mugs. Moose poured the beer as the mug frosted over with just the right head of foam.

"Fifty cents."

The man paid and took a large gulp. No one chatted him up, and he seemed content to sit and rest his forearms on the bar, his shoulders hunched.

I turned back to my cup of coffee, and the neon lights from the beer

signs mingled with the blue fluorescent tubes around the edge of the
ceiling. The pink and green palm trees labeled "Oasis" shone through
the front window. The jukebox kept playing that Elvis song, "Are You
Lonesome Tonight." The air, thick with cigarette smoke, spilt beer, and
Charter, formed a miasma that hung suspended over us. Jesse and Robert
laughed at some lame joke, and Max drummed his fingers against the
bar as he leaned over and looked at the man. Victoria Maness and her
latest sidekick slid in the door about then, and all thought of the stranger
melted in the sticky atmosphere.

Catfish offered me a ride home a little later, but something told me
to stay a bit longer. Then near closing time I heard the guy ask Moose
where Edna was. Moose shrugged his shoulders. "Around, who's asking?"

The man didn't take the bait. He waited a few beats and then said,
"Tell her it's about Bad Eye."

Moose had been around for a while. He had owned a few places
himself, and he had seen it all. Well over six feet tall with salt and pepper
hair, his face showed the years of late nights and hard drinking. He was
nobody's fool or nervous messenger boy, either. He waited a few minutes
and then took the dolly from the corner and went to the back to start
loading the coolers. Johnny and I watched the stranger, who sat and
waited and drank.

Moose reappeared with four cases of beer and began filling the
coolers. He worked silently with the rhythm of repetition. The bottles
clanked as he laid them on their sides, and after one cooler was filled, he
announced to the clientele, "Last call."

The patrons checked their drinks, and some started to look for car
keys and money. The women waved for one more drink each. This was
usually when I began my walk back home. But for some reason I thought
I might hang around and see if anything happened. The stranger just sat.
Casually, as if he couldn't care less if dead lice fell off him, Moose leaned
over and said, "Edna'll be here 'bout closing."

Thirty minutes later, everyone had shuffled out but Moose, Johnny,
me, and the man. Edna pulled up in her Caddy. Johnny began closing the
blinds and dousing the Schlitz sign. He turned off the Oasis palm trees
as Edna came in the front door. She nodded to me. Moose stepped into

the back room, but I could still feel his presence there behind the door.
Edna sauntered over to the guy.

"You looking for me?"

"Heard Bad Eye owed you money."

"Yep."

"You want to collect?"

Edna placed her hand on the bar and leaned that way. "Always try to
collect my debts."

At that, the man moved closer, and I saw Edna tense up.

"We've got Bad Eye," he said so low Edna turned her head to look at
him. I leaned in a little closer, too.

"You what?"

"We've got him."

"You holding him somewhere?"

"Maybe."

Edna swung her purse up on the bar. "Is he okay? Not that I care."

"Yeah, right now he is."

"So why are you holding him?"

The man picked up his glass and took a last sip. "We need something
from him. You might could help us."

"Why should I?"

"Then I'd help you get your money." His hands cupped the mug. He
looked straight ahead.

"Hold on. I'm not that desperate. I don't need any run-in with the law."

"We'd fix it where you wouldn't be."

He still didn't look at Edna. I kept my head down, trying to hear
every word.

"I don't know. Let me think."

"We don't have a lotta time to think. Are you in or not?" He turned
and looked at Edna then.

Edna looked over at me, and I caught that look in her eyes. Edna
Love had always been a gambler. When she was younger, she wouldn't
hesitate to pitch in and try something. She had lost money, lovers, and
friends doing the unexpected, but she liked the thrill of it. I could see
that adrenaline rush just now lure her. There was a secret buried in there,

and she loved secrets. She looked at me and raised her eyebrows. I just shrugged.

"Okay, but I'm taking my baby sister with me." She motioned toward me, and the hair stood up on the back of my neck. The man leaned forward, looked at me, and said fine.

"Let's go." He got up, laid a five-dollar bill on the counter, and started out the door. Edna looked in the mirror, patted her hair, and hollered to Moose, "Lock up, hon."

She teetered on her high heels as she looped her arm through mine. We climbed into the back seat of the man's car, and I figured this was the end of me and Nuanz. He shut the car door for us, and we saw Johnny waiting in the shadows under the awning.

"See ya, John," Edna tossed over her shoulder at him.

"Be careful," he mouthed as he watched us drive off.

Bad Eye went missing every once in a while. I had heard more about Bad Eye than I had actually seen. He terrorized people, especially the vulnerable, with his bad temper and cussing. He was a tall man—skinny as a rake—with light brown skin and wild, tangled hair. His wandering right eye was milky-like with a shade of blue like an early morning sky. It was always cocked about forty-five degrees northwest of where he was headed. His real name was Zeke Monroe, but he claimed his mama named him Bad Eye. The nickname stuck because he claimed he could put the bad eye on folks if they crossed him. That happened more than you would think. Sometimes kids would tie firecrackers onto his dog's tail or dare each other to touch the side of his house and call his name. I learned bits and pieces of the Bad Eye legend from my customers at the cafe and occasional references Edna would make.

Bad Eye rented one of Edna's houses down on East End and always seemed to be a month or two behind. He drove an ancient, flatbed truck rusted out to a dull red with a missing window on the passenger side. The sign on the side of his truck said, "Will haul off anything." He collected junk all over the county, and his truck always had a load of something tied down with rope and leaning to the side. Piles of old tin, scraps of machinery, rusted nails, or anything missing a part—Bad Eye would take it off your hands and then resell it for salvage. We knew something wasn't right 'cause his truck hadn't moved from in front of the AAA Bail Bond place for over a week. Of course, Edna was looking for her money more than for Bad Eye himself.

As we drove into the country, the moonlight bathed the fields, bare trees, and ditches. The clear, cold air made the stars shine brighter. About a mile outside of Nuanz, we turned off onto Gumwoods Road. The man made no pretense of our not knowing where we were going. Could be he didn't care. Could be we would never see anybody again anyway. After Edna's first sentence—"My mama told me never to ride with a stranger"—got no response, Edna decided to sit tight. She patted me on my leg, to reassure me, I guess, and winked. I knew then she probably had a plan.

We pulled down into a pasture with a gate that wasn't even locked. The man left it open, and we bounced across the field to a little, abandoned cabin underneath a stand of trees. The weeds were knee-high, and there was another car pulled to the side with its taillight showing. I couldn't make out the car's make or color. The lights were dim through the cabin windows.

We walked up onto the wooden porch, and the man knocked on the door—three solid raps. We heard a key turn, and the door opened to a tall, mulatto man with kinky, red hair, a wide face with acne scars, and a big, bulbous nose. Edna didn't say a word, but I could tell she was getting a little keyed up. She slung her purse tighter against her left side. That seemed to comfort her. I tried not to throw up.

There in the corner, tied to an old, straight chair, was Bad Eye. He looked even crazier than usual. Sitting at the wooden kitchen table was a young black girl—familiar in some way—she was light-skinned with peroxide streaks through her wide Afro. She was dealing out a game of solitaire, and there was a half-smoked cigarette in the overflowing ashtray by her hand. Everybody looked at each other. Finally Edna said, "Bad Eye, what's going on?"

He scrunched up his lips and his bad eye. He shook his head.

"Bad Eye, I've come all the way out here in the middle of the night. What's going on?"

"Ain't nothing going on."

No one said a word. Edna walked across the room and stood between Bad Eye and the girl.

"Yeah, something's going on, and I wanna know what." Edna crossed her arms, jutted out her left hip, and started tapping her right foot.

Still nothing. Bad Eye's shirt was missing; there was dried blood around his mouth, but he didn't seem too much the worse for wear.

I watched the girl lay a red queen on a black king and turn over her first ace. The big, redheaded guy pointed at me and asked, "Wanna sit?" I collapsed onto the first chair available. Edna kept standing.

"I wanna talk, and if I don't hear somebody telling me something, my ride's gonna be here in about ten minutes flat."

Big Red started in. "Bad Eye put a hex on Pookie."

His voice trembled a bit as he said the name. Edna bit her bottom lip to keep from smiling.

"And who is Pookie?"

"My baby brother."

"How do you know Bad Eye put a hex on Pookie?"

"'Cause Bad Eye said he was going to. And then Pookie started getting the shaky leg thing and his head hurt and he was throwing up all day and night."

Bad Eye growled and tilted the chair back on its legs.

"And what am I supposed to do about that?" asked Edna.

"Well, since Bad Eye owes you, I thought you could call him in on the hex—you know—since you got some power over him."

Edna stalled for a moment as if she was really thinking about it. "I don't know how that works exactly."

"To undo a hex you got to have some power over the conjurer."

Edna uncrossed her arms and quit tapping her foot. She wandered over toward the girl and watched her lay a red seven on the black eight.

"Why dontcha just shoot him?"

Bad Eye slammed the chair down hard and started mumbling. "Ain't nobody gonna be shooting Bad Eye. No way. No how. Naw, it ain't gonna happen. You sons a bitches can try to shoot me but it ain't gonna happen. I gots people know where I am. And they gonna come after you. Yeah, uh-huh, ain't nobody gonna be shooting . . ."

About that time Big Red took the butt of his gun and cracked it across Bad Eye's skull. I had the urge to get up and run like hell, but I stayed still.

"Now hold on here." Edna swung her purse in front of her and eased her hand inside.

Red looked at her. "I been listening to him for a week now, and I've 'bout had it up to here."

"Calm down, everybody." Edna's voice had enough edge to it that we all took a deep breath. "Let's see what we can do here. First of all, where's Pookie?"

"He's not too far from here."

"Can you get him here before daylight?"

Big Red nodded his head.

"Let us talk to Bad Eye in private."

They all looked at each other, and then Big Red shoved his gun back into his pocket. The girl looked up, and Red said, "You too." The three of them walked out on the porch, leaving the door cracked open. I held my hands together to keep them from shaking and didn't say a word.

Edna pulled a chair near to Bad Eye and put her purse on the floor. She leaned over—not too close—and asked him, "Why'd you put a hex on Pookie?"

Bad Eye sat for a minute. "He been acting mannish around my baby girl."

"How old is your baby girl?"

"I dunno for sure, 'bout nineteen or twenty."

"Bad Eye," Edna shook her head to admonish. "You can't keep them away from her at that age using your hoodoo. That's not right and you know it."

Bad Eye looked at the door and then lowered his voice. "I'se really just trying to skeer him a little and he got all taken with it. You know some people take it harder than others, Miss Edna."

"I know, but we need to work something out here. I'm afraid they're going to really hurt you."

Bad Eye gritted his teeth and sighed. "They been talking 'bout that stuff out at Jimson Wells, too. You know where that body was found?

People say you can hear him out there moaning. Now I didn't have nothing to do with that at all."

Edna sat there. "So do you want me to help you or not?"

"All right—see what you can work out."

"You sit here and nod your head, and don't say a word." Edna got up and clomped over to the front door.

"Bring Pookie in, and we'll see what we can do."

The white man left in his car, and Edna sent me out in the yard to wave Johnny over. He was waiting in Edna's car. I told him to pull over and wait. Johnny parked and propped his feet up on the dash for a quick nap. Inside, the girl finished her game of solitaire. Everybody was waiting for Pookie. About ten minutes later, a set of headlights bounced across the pasture, and the car pulled up close to the front porch.

Pookie climbed out of the passenger side of the car. He looked like he was about twenty years old, a little darker than Big Red, with his hair straightened and parted on the side. He was big, as in running back big, with a neck as thick as a gatepost. He had to be well over six feet tall with broad shoulders and big hands. He looked sick, though. His belt was cinched extra tight, and the top of his pants was all bunched together like he had lost a lot of weight. There was a pallor underneath his skin, and his eyes looked weak when he looked at Edna. He couldn't seem to pick up his feet, and his loafers flapped against his white socks as he stepped onto the porch.

"Pookie, this is Miss Edna Love."

"Hello, Pookie. I been talking to Bad Eye and we're gonna try to work something out, but you got to promise me you'll do exactly as I say and not mess with his daughter anymore."

Pookie looked like he was going to throw up when Edna said Bad Eye's name. He clutched his shirt in his left hand, and his right hand made the sign as he covered his eyes. "Whatever you say. I gotta have some relief here."

Everything was quiet then. The sky was not as dark as before.

"Red, before we start I got a couple of things I need to know," Edna said.

"Okay."

"First of all, y'all got anything to do with that dead man at Jimson Wells? 'Cause if you do, I'm out of here."

"Oh, God, naw, Miss Edna. Me and Pookie had some business over near Jimson Wells last week that we had to take care of."

"You're not trying to blame that on Bad Eye, too?"

"Well, you see, Pookie had been feeling bad for about three days with a headache and seeing jagged lights when he shut his eyes. And while we was out that way near the Wells, we got to talking about that killing." He looked over at Pookie. "It all started going worse and it seemed like that may have been Bad Eye's fault, too. So we thought we might oughta try to lay that on him, you know, to maybe get him picked up and get the hex off of Pookie."

Pookie stared at the floor and never even lifted his head.

"But then we thought of you. Now don't be trying to use that Jimson Wells thing against us 'cause it might backfire and . . ."

Big Red's voice trailed off, and I could see his hands balled up in a fist.

"Okay, I understand. I just wanted to be sure." Edna continued, "Now all I know about releasing a hex is that both parties have to participate in some way, and with a go-between both parties have to agree to the transfer going through that person. Agree?"

Bad Eye nodded his head. Pookie stood there trembling with his eyes still covered and nodded his head, too.

"Here's what we're gonna do. Pookie, sit down."

Edna reached into her ample bosom and took out a cramped handkerchief. "Bad Eye's gonna spit on this handkerchief, and I will place it on Pookie's head, his chest, and his stomach. Then Pookie has to get rid of it by throwing it into some water—like a pond or the river or something. Since I am assuming this transfer, then both parties have to pay back the debt owed me. So Pookie, Bad Eye, each of you put $200 in a brown paper bag and leave it on my doorstep no later than Thursday night. If I don't get two bags of cash, then I'm going straight to the sheriff. Understood?"

Everyone nodded.

Edna handed the hankie to Bad Eye. He spat into it with all his might. She crossed the room and, carefully holding the corners, placed the handkerchief on Pookie's forehead, his chest, and then his belly. It was dead quiet. Nobody was even breathing hard.

Pookie's head started shaking like he had the Saint Vitus dance, and he wiped the sweat off his face with the crook of his arm, keeping the sign in front of his body the whole time. His knee bobbed up and down, and his heel made a sound on the floor like the drum of a turkey on a hollow log. Edna took the white handkerchief and spread it on the table. The ashtray was full, and she dumped the ashes into the middle of the kerchief, placed the glass ashtray on top, and tied the ends together. Boy, is she good, I thought.

She dropped the bundle unceremoniously into Pookie's lap.

"Sink this into some deep water tonight, and you should feel better tomorrow."

Then she looked at Big Red. "Now if you'd untie Bad Eye, then we'll give him a ride into town."

The sky was quickly turning from gray to pink to full light. Johnny pulled the car over and stopped at the end of East End Street, and Bad Eye opened the front door.

"'Bout that money, Miss Edna."

"Have it there Thursday, Bad Eye. I mean it. Hell, I just saved your sorry black ass."

Bad Eye laughed, "Maybe you did," and slammed the car door.

Edna sighed, kicked off her shoes, and rubbed her swollen feet against her legs. She pulled me over and gave me a hug.

"Now see, hon. You never know what the day might bring."

"Home, James," she said to Johnny with a hint of a smile on her beautiful lips. "I only doubled the return on my money, but law, I had ten times the fun."

My bed had never looked so good. Before I crawled between the covers, I spat twice between two of my fingers to be on the safe side.

A Balm in Gilead

A few days after the rescue, I was trying not to think about home and Christmas. When Grace knocked on Room 404 at the Nuanz Motor Inn, I was glad to see her.

"Come on in. Don't just stand there." I motioned her over to the foot of my bed and sat back in my chair.

She closed the door and huddled in her thin coat. Her bony wrists stuck out of her sleeves and the buttons were missing from the coat.

"Where's your cap and gloves?"

She glared at me. "I don't need no cap and I always lose one glove."

I nodded and unfolded the newspaper on the table. We began our usual conversation.

"Whatcha been up to?"

"Nothing."

"Anything going on in town?"

She shrugged her shoulders.

"How's the spy game going?"

She rolled her eyes and looked at me. "Somebody's spying on you."

My ears pricked up. "Me? Who, you?"

"Nope," she said. "I've seen him a couple of times when you weren't here—a man standing against those trees across the road." She walked over to the window.

"What's he look like?"

"I dunno—an old man."

"Did he see you?"

"Of course not. You think I'm crazy?"

I felt hollow inside. "Why do you think he's spying on me?"

Grace paused and looked out. "I don't know, but he was staring at your door."

"Well, had you ever thought I might need to know?"

She didn't answer me.

"You need to come get me if you see him again." I started to say more but then let it go.

"How's school?"

"We get out for Christmas tomorrow."

She wandered around my room, picking up my books and staring into my open closet.

"I know. It's also the winter solstice—the shortest day of the year."

She turned to me. "So what happens on the winter solstice?"

"Well, the sun is as far away as it can be. People used to think the sun was disappearing. They would try and bring it back. They would light bonfires on the hills, and roll burning wheels down the road. Some would stay up all night tending a fire and praying the sun would come back. When it did, they would celebrate. They thought they had saved the sun from dying."

"So I need to stay in tomorrow night and light a fire?" she asked with just the right amount of little girl sarcasm.

"Yeah, that would be a great idea."

I turned to the classified ads on the last page. Puppies for Christmas.

"Have you heard anything about the investigation?"

Grace reached into my closet and turned on the light. "Who would tell me anything? How 'bout you?"

I kept reading the paper. "Maybe there was something else going on."

"Like what?"

"I don't know. There had been some fights in the clubs that week."

Grace leaned against the table and picked up the salt shaker. "That woman went missing, too."

I looked up from the paper. "What woman?"

"You ever hear about that black man that was killed at Jimson Wells?"

Oh, Lord, I thought. "Yeah."

"He used to meet a white woman down at Rem's."

"When?"

"Lots of times. They were there a few nights before the solstice."

"Who else saw this?"

"Me and Noah and a man in an old truck. He threw a bottle at them when they left. But he couldn't see us. We were hiding underneath the bush."

"Girl, you are going to get in trouble with all this spying."

"It's something to do."

She put her hands on her hips and stretched up on her tiptoes to see herself in my mirror.

"Besides, I can't sleep at night anyway."

I shut up then. She was ready to take off.

"So got your Christmas shopping done?"

"We don't have Christmas at my house."

"Sure you do."

"Aunt Virginia doesn't even know what day it is."

"Well, why don't we do some window shopping at least? Maybe tomorrow after I get off work?"

She gave me that look and tried not to smile.

"We'll go look and then stop at the five-and-dime. My treat."

The next day we met in town. Strings of colored lights lined the law office windows, the banks had trees in their lobbies, and wreaths were on all the shop doors. The hardware store even had one of those new aluminum Christmas trees with the rotating multicolored lights. We stood and watched the cycle of blue, red, green, and yellow lights as people passed by and headed home. Grace and I stopped at Mr. Flowers's jewelry store. The whole store was only about six feet wide. We stared at the diamond necklaces and birthstone rings in the window display. I asked Grace when her birthday was.

"June, I think," she said.

"Whadda ya mean, think?" I asked. "Don't you know when your own birthday is?"

"Aunt Virginia doesn't know for sure."

"Sure she does. She's got your birth certificate, doesn't she?"

"Nope. Can't find it anywhere."

Mr. Flowers came over and waved at us. We waved back.

"Where were you born?"

"I dunno. Mama left me here with Aunt Virginia when I was about three, she thinks."

"How'd you get in school?"

"I don't know. I make up a birthday whenever they ask."

Our conversation was fogging up the window. We stepped back.

"So what did you pick this year?"

"March 15."

"Beware the Ides of March," I muttered.

"Is that a bad day? Do I need to change it?"

"No, it was just a bad day for somebody named Julius."

We began walking again. "So when's your birthday, Meshac?"

"Who cares?"

We wandered through the five-and-dime and picked out what we would buy if we had money. I chose some red plastic roses and a warm brown sweater. Grace picked a flashlight and a packet of ball and jacks. We tried on some hats, and I told her she needed a baby doll. When Mrs. Grady began following us around, we laughed and raced out the door.

I walked halfway down College Street toward the playground with Grace and watched as she took the shortcut through the playground to her house. Then I turned and walked quickly back toward the motel.

The gray day became desperately dark. Inside my room I stood without the lights on with my palm against the windowpane, watching and thinking. I stared at the trees across the way. Perhaps it was time for me to move on. I closed my eyes and felt suspended, as if my feet dangled over emptiness. I held on tightly to a rope that swung over the gully from Wicket and ended on the courthouse spire in Nuanz. I might not ever see Irene or Roy or any of my friends again. Joe didn't seem that interested in me. Why should I stay?

The seasons were passing, and the planets kept spinning. Old Man Winter was on his way. December 21. Each day forward there would be a little more light. Those folks long ago must have felt some power over their lives when the sun reappeared after their nightlong vigil. Yep, we brought the sun back. Maybe the winter solstice was about hope. Putting things right was getting harder, though.

"Hey, old girl, don't be so quickiefied. Maybe I'll hit the road. Before another birthday comes around."

Christmas Day was not so bad. Edna organized a meal for us derelicts—me, Aunt Virginia, Grace, Catfish, and Johnny. I asked Loretta to come, but she had family. None of us could cook, of course, so we took leftovers from the Christmas Eve special at the Bluebird.

I was surprised at the number of folks who turned up to eat at the cafe on Christmas Eve. There were lots of people who didn't have anybody to share Christmas with. Louise and I were hopping from eleven thirty till two o'clock.

Several of my good customers were there: Mr. Smith, Lawyer Malone, the Hays couple, and the Dennison sisters. From the little gray-haired ladies to the balding, straight-backed farmers, it was a nice assortment. We all knew we didn't have any family, but we could soak up a little Christmas cheer here at the cafe.

Edd Biggs, the skinflint, even left Louise a tip. He nodded his head as he left and I sang out, "Merry Christmas." He was a weird little man who gave me a creepy-crawly feeling. I rarely saw him, but at times I could feel his squinty eyes on me. He was a loner, they said, since his wife died a few years ago.

Rob Adams locked the doors when the last lingering customer left, and I divvied up the leftovers. Rob and Louise were eating with family, so I got my choice of food for Edna's crowd. I loaded up the chicken and dressing, green bean casserole, creamed corn, and sweet potatoes. There was a pan of rolls. Surely Edna could bake a pan of rolls. I had hidden one of Mrs. Roberts's homemade pies in the back of the walk-in refrigerator. Edna came by to pick me up, and Rob actually helped load the goodies. We took the goodies to Edna's and stored them in her empty refrigerator. I started to spend the night at Edna's, but I thought that was going a little overboard. She didn't pressure me.

My motel room was dark when I got there. The Christmas moon was full, and I could see 404 shining on my door. The Nuanz Motor Inn sign lit up the front corner of the complex. The red and blue lights spilled a welcome of sorts to travelers. The vacancy light was permanently on. I could hear the hum of the neon like background music. I wasn't doing too bad here, alone. Nuanz felt kind of like home. At least there was no George leering at me and touching Irene. If evil was close, I was still upright. Maybe I could stay a little longer.

Suddenly the hum was broken by voices and laughter. Christmas caroling? Jeez Louise. . . . My tiny room was warm and cozy. I had no chimney for St. Nick, so there was no need to hang a stocking. Sugarplums would be welcomed, though, as I settled in for the night and slept a dreamless sleep on Christmas Eve.

Christmas Day with Edna Love was about what I expected. After a cup of coffee and a shower, I walked over to Edna's house around eleven. No one else dared to appear until after noon. Edna was dressed in her best red outfit with tinsel in her hair and long, dangly Christmas ornaments on her ears. I expected her to light up and say "Merry Christmas" somewhere. There was a tiny tree on the hearth in her den with the artificial firelight in the grate behind it. Gifts were piled all around, dwarfing the tree with their shiny paper and satiny bows. We began dividing the food to heat up, and I set the table in the dining room. We had to shove a few piles of papers and clothes into the corners or under the nearest bed to make room. Living alone, we tend to let things pile up like that.

Aunt Virginia and Grace arrived around twelve thirty. Virginia had a scowl on her face and shoved a jar of homemade pickles and a loaf of white bread at me when they walked through the door. Grace hopped from one foot to another, chattering nonstop. I caught her reading the name tags on the gifts.

"I didn't know there would be presents," she said.

"Of course, how can you have Christmas without presents?" Her eyes were shining. "But first we eat."

By the time it was all ready, Catfish Somers and Johnny Crenshaw had arrived. We had a full table, and the meal began. The food was delicious, warm, and filling. Catfish could hardly eat for telling so many tales. Grace pecked at her plate like a bird with one eye trained on the den and the presents. Finally we pushed back from the table, and I began clearing the plates. Catfish stopped me. "Now you women go in there and open your presents. Me and Johnny will clean up." Johnny looked surprised but willing. The four women went into the den.

Edna asked Grace to give out the presents. The first one went to Aunt Virginia. She acted as if she couldn't take it.

"We didn't bring any presents." She folded her arms.

Edna shushed her. "This is all my doing, Virginia. Now be nice."

She rolled her eyes and stuck her long legs out in front of her. "Whatever."

Grace distributed the gifts to everyone—four boxes for each of us. That left Grace's under the tree. I could see her counting them as she set them over on the floor beside her aunt. I had hidden Edna's earlier and whispered to Grace where to find it. She ran back with it and laid it beside Edna's pile.

"Shall we open one at a time and take turns or go for it?" I asked innocently.

"Go for it," shouted Edna and Grace together. Paper, ribbons, and boxes flew. A small whirlwind was let loose there as oohs, aahs, and "look at this" bounced off the walls. For the next half hour or so, it was Christmas at Edna Love's, and all was sweet and peaceful. O Holy Night.

My granny and Daddy used to love Christmas, too. When Granny lived with us, she would make homemade boiled custard and coconut cake if we had the money. One Christmas my older brothers were roughhousing in the kitchen, and Tom got pushed into the middle of the cake. We all ran and hid, knowing somebody was going to get a licking. That coconut cake still tasted good. We always had something we could call Christmas. Some years were better than others, of course, until Daddy died. After he was gone, I tried to play Santa for Irene and Roy. We managed to get by better than some others maybe.

Grace thanked everyone without any prompting. She settled in with her presents in the corner. I gave her a diary with a key, and she held that in her lap. Aunt Virginia tried on her house shoes and a sweatshirt that said "Go Falcons." I actually got a pair of shoes—real shoes—as in black suede flats with a gold buckle. I didn't know where I would ever wear them, but I loved them. Edna was the most surprised when she opened hers. She found a little black book with gold lettering: *Edna's Secrets*. She laughed so long I thought she might choke and then said in a wheezy voice, "Law, hon, I can't begin to write all that down."

I begged her, "Please write it down and leave it to me in your will."

By the time we had cleaned up, the lemon meringue pie was calling us. The adults added a glass of boiled custard with the "flavoring" supplied by Johnny. The afternoon was creeping into night. Aunt Virginia and Grace were the first to leave, and Catfish offered me a ride, but I said I would stay a while longer.

Edna and I settled into our places in the den. The Christmas tree looked especially forlorn now without the presents. The silence was nice.

"Well, hon, merry Christmas. Not too bad, huh?"

"I think it was a very nice Christmas," I said.

"Are you homesick?"

"Maybe a little. But I'll get over it."

Edna kicked off her shoes. "Want me to tell you a story?"

"Sure."

"Let's have a glass of sherry with the storytelling." Edna went to her sideboard and pulled out the crystal bottle with two tiny glasses. I felt like Miss Astor.

"Do I hold my pinkie out to drink this?"

She snorted. "Of course you do."

Edna leaned back in her chair and sipped a bit of the sherry. "So you wanna know Edna's secrets?" She had that gleam in her eye.

"Course I do. Who wouldn't?"

She smiled and nodded her head in agreement. "Well, hon, prop your feet up and let me tell you about a guy I met a long time ago. Freddie Garcia."

I leaned back and let her words pour over me. Boy, was I in for a grand time. I just knew it.

"This all happened before you were even born. I don't recall the exact year but I had been on my own for a while. Daddy died when I was twenty-two—shot by one of his customers, but that's another story—and this thing with Freddie was a few years later. Mama was lingering. She still dressed every day, but it took her to midafternoon to get her face fixed and her clothes on. I kept a bedroom and some clothes in our old house, but I had my own place, too. A little house on a woods lot about a mile out in the country."

Edna's voice softened, and she looked at the Christmas tree shining in the dark. I leaned my head back and balanced the sherry glass on my knee.

"Freddie Garcia. What a dear, sweet, meaner-than-hell, low-down scoundrel he was. He appeared in town one day, and everybody took notice. I was working at the shirt factory making nothing at all 'cause it was based on production. My girlfriends and I were at the drive-in one night when Freddie appeared in this dilapidated Plymouth with no muffler. It was so loud we all just stared at him as he rode up and down the gravel hills trying to find a speaker stand that worked. When he finally stopped his car in front of ours, he forgot to turn off his lights. We started joking about why he kept hitting the brakes every few minutes. Finally I sneaked up and looked in his window. Thought he was asleep and then he turned and looked right at me. Scared the bejesus out of me. But I still remember those luscious brown eyes."

She stood up and freshened our drinks. I began to feel a little woozy.

"The next time I saw Freddie, we were at the skating rink. He came over real polite-like to me and said, 'Pardon me, don't I know you?' I shook my head no and walked off. That got his goat.

"After a few more miss-and-meet encounters, I gave in and started dating Freddie. I fell really hard. He was tall, with those dark brown eyes, and his laughter would wrap around me and skid all the way down to my toes. He was a smooth talker and dance—Lawd, could he ever move. When we took the floor, people would back off and let us go. I can still feel the sweat rolling down my spine as we moved our bodies together in perfect time. We would try anything and laugh and cut up."

She looked at me and I had to ask: "So was he the first?" She squinted her eyes.

"Well now, I can't tell you all my secrets," she smiled, "but at that time he was the best."

I closed my eyes. Her voice brought me back to the present.

"This is where the story turns."

I took another sip of my sherry and tried to see what time it was. I hated to fall asleep in the middle of this. I shook my head and took a breath. "So what happened?"

"I made a big mistake. I let my heart lead my gut. Of course, then I didn't know better, but I had no one to confide in. We were dating exclusive, I thought. He knew my daddy had left us rental property and two bars. I kept working at the factory to keep up appearances, and Clyde, the bar manager, kept the business end going. Then Freddie started making suggestions about how we could make more money. Dumb me, I just wanted him to be happy. I would nod my head and say, 'Sure, go ahead.' He started bartending the Do Drop Inn, making the night deposits."

Edna rolled her eyes. "Then he started stopping in at Mama's house, waiting for me to get off work, he said. Well, you know where this is going. I came home one day and Mama was huddled on the couch crying. 'Mama,' I said, 'what's the matter?'

" 'It's gone. All of it—it's gone.' She pointed into Daddy's office. I ran in there and saw the wall safe standing wide open."

Edna looked at me, and I saw the anger still.

"Empty. Freddie took all the gold coins and silver dollars my granddaddy had saved, plus a stack of cash that would choke a mule. He left me one twenty-dollar bill—lying there all alone, mocking me. I cried like a baby. Turned out he had been shorting the deposits, too. But the worst thing was Annabel Lucas left town with him."

"So what'd you do? Did the sheriff go after him?"

"Well, hon, you see, back then I couldn't exactly explain to the sheriff what a wad of cash and coins was doing in my daddy's safe. I mean, people knew what my daddy had done, but since he died, Mama and me had just been getting by. I didn't know anything about running a business. We let Clyde tell us what to do."

"I am so sorry, Edna."

She laughed. "Don't be. Best lesson I ever learned. Yep, made me who I am today. Smart-ass, beautiful, independent, lonely-at-times Edna Love. But I go to sleep at night and know I am going to be all right."

Then she reached up and took out one of her ornamental chopsticks from her hair. "Here's the secret—shhh, you can't tell a soul: see this?"

She tapped the glittery stick on her knee. "This one I named Freddie. I say his name every day when I place this in my hair." She held the stick in front of her face and spoke to it: "Freddie, you beast you. I'm riding high, how 'bout you?" She laughed.

"I carved his initials in it, see?" She leaned toward me and twirled the black enameled hair ornament in her fat fingers until I saw those scratches. "I burned that twenty dollars, too, and scattered it in the wind."

Then she grinned. "You know, kiddo. You're the only one that can save yourself. Won't anybody do it for you. Can't tell you how. Gotta figure it out for yourself."

She leaned back and aimed the ornament in the right place on the crown of her head. "Yep, this one's for evil. This one's for good."

She nodded her head from one side to the other. "I'll tell you about the other another time."

I nearly said, "I know all about evil," but the words stuck in my throat. I unwound my legs and stood up from the couch to go home. Outside, the cold cleared my head. What a Christmas this had been. I walked home with no fear—only a full stomach and a happy heart. The lights at the Nuanz Motor Inn said, "Welcome home."

Winter settled in and covered us. The cold forced people to quicken their steps and shorten their conversations. They waited for the best parking space at the grocery store, found excuses to skip church, and even when they ventured a trip to the Bluebird Cafe, it wasn't the same. Each one burrowed a little deeper into his snug tunnel and vowed to make it until the seed catalogs arrived in the mail.

As the old Negro spiritual says, could the "wounded be made whole?" Could you "heal a sin-sick soul?" Was there a balm in Nuanz or was it just numbness—not knowing and not caring to know?

Should I Stay or Should I Go?

Joe was off the boat for the first two weeks of the new year. It felt like things were changing between Joe and me. I knew things were going to be different, but I didn't know exactly how. He wanted me to go on a date—like a real date in his car. I balked. I wanted to be a normal kind of girl, but there was something that still pulled at me inside when I thought I was over it. It being George.

But I finally gave in and agreed to go out with Joe on Friday night. "Yes," I said, "on a date."

He grinned at me sitting there at the lunch counter. Then he reached over and touched my face. I leaned away from him. He slapped a dollar down beside his coffee and said, "Be ready at seven sharp," and winked at me. I turned my back on him, but my heart was jumping out of my chest.

When I got off work, I dressed quickly in my one good outfit. The black suede flats looked nice. I could have used a slug of Edna's sherry if I had the nerve to ask for it. Looking in my mirror, I saw a slight resemblance to my mama. Was it my hair or the shape of my face? That was a first. It must have been the scarf I had knotted around my neck. She used to wear those when she dolled up. I untied it and threw it onto the bed. I checked my purse again and wondered if I could get Daddy's gun in there without anybody noticing. At seven, I heard a car pull up. I rushed out before he could even knock. He started around to open the car door for me, but I beat him to it.

"I can open the door myself," I said a little too loud. Watch it, Meshac.

He slid into the front seat and started the car. It was cold, and the heater was not warm yet. There was dried mud in the floorboard, and his work boots and a hammer were lying underneath my feet.

"Here, let me get that out of the way." He leaned over toward me, and I put my foot down.

"No, that's fine. I like having the hammer where I can reach it." Shit, did I say that out loud?

He looked at me and shrugged his shoulders. "Suit yourself."

He shifted gears as we pulled out on the street. I could see my breath and the windows fogged over as the heater cranked up.

"Where are we going on this big date?" Why was I so hateful, I wondered. He looked at me, but then he smiled.

"You'll never guess."

I waited a moment and told myself to calm down and have some fun, dammit.

"Hope it's not the Bluebird Cafe. I hear they have lousy waitresses."

He laughed. "Nope. Try again."

"It's too cold for the drive-in."

He didn't say a word.

"I don't skate anymore. You wanna play some pool at Pierce's?"

He shook his head. I got quiet then.

"There's this new place to eat that's about halfway to Jackson. They serve pizza."

I hated to show my ignorance but what the hell. "What's pizza?"

He kept looking straight ahead. "Something kind of new around here. Ever heard of Chef Boyardee pizza?"

I shook my head no and looked out the window.

"Well, this is all the doings in the big cities. We are going to eat a pizza at Tony's Pizza Place."

I leaned back and tried to relax. "Sounds good to me. I always like an adventure or two."

We sailed on through the darkness, just us two. The headlights whittled the way to who knew what. When we got there, the parking lot was jammed with cars and trucks. The drab frame building was lit up, and the sign above the door said Tony's Pizza. When we stepped inside, the smell of bread and garlic hit me square in the face. I actually felt good. I can do this, I thought.

We squeezed into a booth. The talk was loud, and the music even louder. There were mostly young people here. I saw a young, olive-skinned man behind the counter. He was smiling, and his arms were covered with flour up to his elbows. Suddenly he picked up a circle of dough and tossed it between his hands. He watched it and then twisted it up into the air. It floated there for a few seconds, and we all said, "Ooh, look," before he caught it and laid it gently on a flat, round pan. I am sure you could see the wonder on my face.

Joe grinned and said, "That's our supper."

It was a night of firsts for me. First pizza, first beer (which I really didn't take to), first real date. It felt so damn normal. Joe did most of the talking between bites. He wolfed down twice as much as me. Here in the little pizza place with the steamed-up windows and the chatter of happiness, I even felt pretty.

On the way home, we played the radio loud. When Jerry Lee Lewis came on, it was like he was playing our song. I didn't deserve to be this dang happy, but maybe I could be for a while. The ride back passed quicker than going. We didn't talk much, just listened to WLS and Dick Biondi. But I could feel how near Joe was. I could easily reach across and touch him. His hands looked big and strong there resting on the steering wheel. We seemed to be wrapped in a tight cocoon falling through a dark space. I concentrated on the black asphalt and the path the car lights made. I wanted him to slow down, but I was afraid to say anything. Then we pulled back into the motel lot, and suddenly I wished I had my gun. This helpless feeling made me lightheaded. All I could think about was getting inside—by myself.

He turned off the motor, and I fumbled for the door handle. We both said together, "Well . . ." and then we laughed. I took a breath.

"Thanks for my first ever pizza." I couldn't look at him.

"You're welcome. Thanks for going with me," he paused, "in the car."

I turned and looked into his eyes. He smiled until he saw my face.

"What's the matter?"

"I don't know. Everything and nothing."

I felt tears starting and pulled my purse up tight against my chest. I was afraid to say anything.

He touched my shoulder, and I leaned out of his reach against the door. I couldn't look him in the face.

"Leave me alone. It's not worth the trouble. I promise."

I scrambled out of the car, but he beat me to the door.

"Wait a minute, Meshac. What is going on?"

I clenched my jaw and patted my coat pocket for my keys. He reached for me again. I backed away.

"Forget it, Joe. It's not gonna work out. But thanks for trying."

"What'd I do?"

"Nothing, nothing at all. It's all on me. Leave me alone."

I got my motel door open and slammed it as fast as I could. Then when I heard his car leave, I lay across the bed and cried.

Who did I think I was? You snively little murderer, you.

I avoided Joe for the next few days. Then he left for another six weeks on the boat.

The grayer and colder it got during January, the more I wanted to burrow into my bed. The lure of the Oasis couldn't even overcome my desire to hibernate. Rob Adams at the Bluebird seemed to know that and scheduled me for early mornings the rest of the month. He's like that. Mean. I hated getting up at three in the morning. My attitude probably showed on my face, too. The customers weren't so jolly with me, and I thought my tips were lower. I needed a shot of adrenaline from somewhere. The cold and lack of sunshine even drove Grace inside. She had not been by my room since Christmas. Of course, I was turning in early, too. So I kind of welcomed the knock on my motel door around eight o'clock on Tuesday night. Without even thinking, I flung open the door. It was the sheriff. I froze when I saw him.

"Hiya, Meshac. Can I come in for a minute?"

I couldn't even speak. He sat down in my only chair, and I stood against the wall with my hands behind my back.

"I needed to come by and ask you a few questions, and I didn't think I should do this at the cafe."

My heart was pounding in my throat. I wondered if I was pale.

"What about?" I asked.

"I've had a few calls from a man down in your neck of the woods," he said nonchalantly.

I didn't say a word. Here it is. They've got me now. I forced myself to look at him.

"And?"

"I didn't know exactly where in Mississippi you were from."

"You didn't," I stalled.

"This man was from Greenwood looking for some runaways."

"Runaways?"

"Yeah, some girls had taken off from Greenwood last summer, and their parents were getting kind of desperate to find them." He looked straight at me when he said that.

"That wouldn't be me. I'm not from Greenwood."

He looked at me as if he expected more.

"Besides, my parents are dead," I added.

"Really," he said. "I didn't realize you were on your own. What made you come to Nuanz in the first place?"

"I thought I remembered my daddy's people being from West Tennessee—a place near here."

"Yep." He waited for more.

"But I couldn't figure out exactly where. When I stopped, Edna offered me a job within a few hours and I thought I'd stay for a while and see what there was to do here, you know." Shut up, I thought. Do not say another word.

The sheriff looked at me for a minute and then straightened out both of his legs in front of him as if to relax.

"Well," and he looked back up at me, "guess you're not one of those girls this fellow's looking for then."

"No, sir, I don't think so."

"Okay, Meshac, I just thought I'd ask. You know we don't get many new people in Nuanz—especially young ones. Your name came up."

He folded his fingers down in his right hand and popped each knuckle.

"How much longer are you going to stay?"

"I don't know, Sheriff. Through the winter till spring probably. Then I'll decide."

The sheriff drew his legs back and pushed himself out of the chair. The leather holster squeaked as he shifted his weight to get up.

"You take care now," he said and then waited for me to respond.

I looked him in the eye. "Appreciate it, Sheriff."

My voice was quiet and level, I think. I so wanted him to leave. As the door closed behind him, I stretched out across the bed and pulled the covers over me. I knew for sure now it was time to leave. Too many near misses and warnings these last few months. I pulled out my old backpack and wrapped Daddy's gun with my box of bullets inside my good dress. It didn't take me fifteen minutes to pack everything I owned. I left my extra uniform hanging in the closet. I was paid up to the end of the month here. I needed to get back to Jackson and catch a bus. Probably the best thing would be to go. No explanations, no goodbyes. I hated to mess up Rob Adams but, shit, I needed to get outta here—now. I paced back and forth; that always helped me think. I was spitting cotton my mouth was so dry. Calm down. I would work my shift the next morning and then tell Rob I had to go to Jackson for a day or two. Play it real simple-like.

The Escape

The next day felt longer than usual. The regulars stayed forever, but I kept busy. Edna came by, but she had other things on her mind. Boy, was I going to miss her. Then I heard Mrs. Silverblatt complaining about having to drive her sister-in-law to Jackson. God, what a whiner, but what a chance. When she checked out, I asked if I could hitch a ride with her to Jackson. She acted flabbergasted.

"I guess I'll have room," she finally answered. "I can't take you all over town, though."

"I'll pay for your gas. I'm meeting my auntie and staying the night."

"So it's just one way?"

"Yes, ma'am."

She waited another minute. "Why don't you ride the bus then?"

I looked rather shocked and smiled my sweetest, most sarcastic smile. "Gee, why didn't I think of that?"

Mrs. Silverblatt snorted and closed her purse with a loud click. "Well, you can ride if you want, but the bus goes direct to Jackson at 6 a.m. every weekday."

"Yes, ma'am, I forgot that. That's what I'll do then." Geez.

I couldn't eat any supper that night. I did my laundry before it got dark. Back in my room, I stuffed my clean clothes into my bag and laid out my waitress shoes and extra apron on the bed. Maybe the next wannabe waitress would fit into these shoes. I prayed no one would stop by that night. Rob Adams had swallowed my story. After a mostly sleepless night, I locked the door to Room 404 and laid the key on the office desk. Nothing stirred around me. There was no need to leave a note. That's why it's called an escape. The motel sign lit my way as I walked for the last time toward town. At the taxi stand where the bus tickets were sold, no one was too interested in me. Luckily, there were few passengers at six in the morning. My heart dropped when the bus pulled out of Nuanz. Those were good folks there. I was going to miss them.

I stepped off the bus in Jackson and realized I didn't yet have a plan. Everyone else knew where they were going. As I came out of the terminal, I saw a crowd near the street.

"What's going on?" I asked the woman next to me.

"Oh, that's some of those protesters again." Her eyes narrowed, and she looked pissed off. "If they can't sit in the front of the bus, then they ain't going to ride the bus."

I stood and watched. There were two black men and a black woman walking up and down beside the curb. They had on cardboard signs that said: "Equality for All." The men were in suits with ties and overcoats. One man had on a hat. Their shoes were shined, and the woman was dressed in her Sunday best, too. They looked straight ahead and never said a word as they walked back and forth.

Across the street there were angry white people shouting terrible things. Hoodlums are what my English teacher, Miss Arnold, would have called them. Bareheaded in worn blue jeans with shirttails flying,

one of them waved a sign—"If you don't want to ride our buses, then
walk." People looked as they passed by, but the crowd grew as the insults
got worse. A white woman not much older than me stood with her small
daughter beside her. The mother shouted at the blacks, "Get out of our
town," until her face turned red. The little girl started crying.

"See," she shouted, "see what you done to my baby."

The whites would edge halfway across the street and then pull back.
It was mesmerizing. The mob swayed like a giant snake coiled upon
itself ready to strike. I stood on the outskirts as more black protesters
approached. They, too, were dressed for church. Their faces were solemn
with no expression.

Two policemen arrived and walked up and down between the groups.
The white guys quieted down. "Move along," the police said to both
sides. The whites stood there behind the blue uniforms filled with white
men. The blacks looked straight ahead and paced back and forth. Then I
heard the big cop say to the blacks, "We're gonna have to take y'all down
to the station if you don't move along." One of the black men stopped
and talked with the cop. He then turned and handed the signs to two
other black men standing in the crowd behind him. A police car pulled
up and the three protesters were put into the back seat. The white crowd
cheered. The black men and their signs disappeared.

I headed toward the nearest hotel a few blocks away. I didn't know
what else to do but get a room. The man at the desk turned around to
wait on me.

"I need a room."

He raised his eyebrows and looked me up and down.

"We're full right now."

I stared at him.

He peered at me over his glasses. "Are you from out of town?" as if
being from out of town was a disease.

"Yessir, that's why I need a room."

He looked down for a moment as if trying to decide how best to put
this: "We are full to capacity tonight."

I knew then something wasn't right. "Is there another hotel nearby?"

"They're full, too."

"What's going on?" I tried to say that as nicely as I could.

"You should know. You came in on the bus with the others, didn't you?" I waited.

"We don't have any rooms available. Try the Negro college down the street. Maybe they'll put you up." He turned and walked back into his office. Boy, what in the world was going on?

I walked back out and sat down on the bench outside the courthouse. The pigeons were busy looking for scraps, and people hurried to work. When the stores opened, I went inside and pretended to shop. I was good at that. Finally I decided to go back to the terminal and just buy a ticket out of there. It was nearly noon, and as I approached I saw another crowd gathering to heckle the fresh demonstrators. This time I was standing on the white side.

The talk was even more hateful. I could barely see the black protesters on the other side of the street. They were doing the same thing as this morning—walking and holding signs. I tried to walk around the crowd to get to the terminal, but two young guys stepped up close beside me. Then I heard the yelling begin: "Get out of our town." There was laughter. "You don't need to be riding no bus. You black tar babies. Get out of our town."

Others began shouting, and suddenly the two guys next to me reached into their jackets and lobbed some eggs across the street. They landed with a splat at the curb. This encouraged the crowd as they shuffled forward. A whiff of fear, or was it excitement, floated up from the too-close bodies. They wanted to do something. I, too, could feel the yearning like a magnet pulling them to harm those who were not like them. A girl to my left shouted as she jumped up and down, "Jiggaboo, get back in colored town where you belong."

I tried again to push my way out, but the crowd tightened like a fist. It swelled, expanding in numbers, and grew more ferocious. Someone stepped on my shoe and pulled it off my heel. I tried to reach down and pull it back on. Then someone bumped me, and I fell to my knees. No hands were extended to pull me up, and I backed my way up to standing with my head down.

I kept stepping away, pushing with my elbows through the crowd.

Finally I could see the edge of the crowd thinning, and I nudged my way out. I was standing in no man's land between the two sides.

At that moment, the police arrived again and stood there as the front line of whites stood not two feet away from the marchers. Then the white crowd swayed as if lifted up by an unseen hand. I could see other black students gathered by the entrance to the terminal, watching. The air trembled with the force of a gathering storm. The police shouted over the bullhorn, but the words made no sense. Then eggs and rocks began flying. I covered my head and saw one of the black women protesters hit on the side of the head. Blood trickled down her face. She wavered but did not fall. One of the black men rushed over to her, but she pushed him away.

Then the police waded in between the protesters, pushing against both sides. Suddenly I was surrounded by the black students, and I felt a stinging thud on my shoulder. I turned and saw a white mass of flailing arms and screaming faces. I was pushed to the other side now. So this is what it feels like? I couldn't breathe, and then a white woman pointed at me, and I saw her mouth the words over and over as she shouted: "Nigger lover. Nigger lover. Nigger lover."

Suddenly someone shouted close to me: "Disband, run, go, go, go." I turned and started running with the black students down the street. I could hear sirens and shouting. Everyone around me was running, and I was, too. There were a couple of white boys beside me and then they disappeared. My satchel bounced against my back, but it felt good to be running. I leaned against the side of a building to catch my breath, and a young black woman came up beside me.

"Don't stop here. Come with me."

We heard some shouts and ducked our heads and ran the best we could crouched down. Suddenly I saw an iron railing and some steps leading down into a basement. The girl knocked on the door, and then we were inside surrounded by people, all talking at once. When I came to my senses, I saw a tall white man standing with two older white women near a table. There were coffee, bandages, and Mercurochrome with towels. I saw a plaque on the wall. "Sunday School 185, Offering $34.50." I was in the basement of the Mother Pilgrim Colored Methodist Church. Oh, God, what had I done now?

The girl who brought me to the church looked familiar. She saw me staring at her.

"I saw you that night with Bad Eye and Edna?"

"Yeah," she smiled.

"So you're Big Red's daughter?"

"Granddaughter. What are you doing over here?"

I laughed. "I don't have a clue. I was hanging out, and all of a sudden I started running, too."

The white man came over. "I'm Professor Swafford. Are you with the group from Greenville?"

I shook my head. "No, I'm from Nuanz."

He frowned. "So you're not here to help with the boycott?"

I felt kind of bad. "No, not really. I started running and ended up here."

He blinked and then smiled.

"We'll see you get back safely. Just give us some time."

He motioned for me to get some coffee. Then he and the white women moved to a back table with some black men in whispered conference.

The coffee warmed my insides. My teeth stopped chattering. I sat by myself in a corner. Everyone looked at me without looking at me. I knew I needed to get out of there. After some time passed, I walked over to Big Red's granddaughter.

"Excuse me, I didn't get your name."

She turned and half-smiled. "Oh, I'm Queen—Queen Esther actually, from the Bible." She gave me an eye roll. "I go by Queenie."

"I'm Meshac from the fiery furnace," I said, and she laughed. "Few people get that reference."

"I know how that is." She nodded her head.

"I think I'll walk back downtown now if you'll point me in the right direction."

"Sure." She walked me to the door. "Do you need a ride back to Nuanz?"

Boy, did that sound like a good idea. Before I could think about it, I said yes.

"I've got to pick up some things in town," she said. "We'll leave from the Star Grocery. It's about a mile out of town. Can you get there by four o'clock?"

"Sure. Thanks."

The rest of the afternoon passed slowly. I sat or leaned wherever I could in town that looked safe. I watched the First State Bank building clock. When it struck three, I started walking north on Highway 45. In thirty minutes I saw a concrete block building on the right. The Esso sign was faded, and a small, hand-printed sign in the window said Star Grocery. I could smell the barbecue pit out back. A bell tinkled as I opened the door. Someone shouted from the back, "Be right out."

I waited inside the store. Then a small, brown-faced woman appeared. "Can I help you?"

I was so relieved. "I'm to meet Queen here at four."

"All right. Have a seat if you'd like."

There were a couple of straight-back chairs pulled up to the stove. The lady watched me and then went back to her work chopping barbecue in the kitchen. I could hear the thud of the meat cleaver, and the sweet aroma of the pulled pork made my mouth water. Once I got still, I realized how tired I was. The heat from the stove made my eyes heavy. I must have dozed off. Finally, Queen Esther stuck her head in the door and said, "Let's go."

The lady appeared and smiled at Queenie. "Hey, baby. Can you stay awhile?" She wiped her hands on her apron.

"No, ma'am. We need to head back to Nuanz." Queen gave the lady a quick hug.

"Well, bye, Bookie. Come back now."

I had never ridden in a car with a black person before. "What a day," I said as I climbed into the front seat.

"You don't have a clue, girl."

"Yeah, I know. Sometimes I think I've got all the troubles in the world but then . . ." I shut up.

She shifted gears and handed me a pack of cigarettes. "Get one out for me. Take one yourself if you like."

"I'm too young to smoke." I'm always cracking jokes. I shook out a cigarette and passed it to her. She pulled a lighter out of her pocket. The smoke reminded me of my daddy. I shrugged and noticed a twinge in my left shoulder.

"When I was a little girl, my mama told me, 'You are royalty, Queen Esther.'" She took a long drag from the cigarette.

I didn't say anything.

"I didn't feel like royalty today." She nodded her head and tapped the ashes into the ashtray. She looked at me.

I got the courage to ask a question. "So why were you there?"

Queen took another deep pull on her cigarette. The smoke floated out of her mouth as she answered, "I don't know. I heard about what was going on from some of my friends. I thought I might see if I could help out. Felt like I was supposed to be there. You know, a certain time, a certain place."

She looked straight ahead. A truck pulled around us and zoomed off into the near darkness.

"Big Red don't understand. All he knows to do is keep working for the man and taking care of his family."

"He took care of Pookie, didn't he?"

Queen smiled. "Him and Miss Edna did." She tapped the ashes again and glanced in the rearview mirror. "He means well, he just don't know anything else."

She reached over and turned the radio up. The music faded in and out with static as she rolled the dial through the numbers. She snapped it back off.

I didn't know what to say to that, although I kind of understood her. We both stayed quiet then and watched the sun turn the sky red. It was still January, and night came early.

We didn't try to talk. I was dog-tired and content to travel the next few miles in silence. Then the road narrowed, and the car shuddered a bit as it throttled down through the descending darkness.

As the sun sank and we headed into Nuanz, the streetlights came on one by one as if we lit them as we approached. I thought, "Keep going. Here is where you belong. Here is where you are safe."

"Where do you stay?"

"Nuanz Motor Inn."

She shook her head and smiled. "I better let you out a couple of blocks from there. I got some kinfolks work there."

"Who's that?"

"Loretta. She can get pretty nosy sometimes."

"Tell me about it." I grinned.

Queenie pulled over and I asked, "What do I owe you?"

"Nothing."

"Oh, I want to pay you something."

"Nope. I was headed this way anyway."

I opened the door and put my foot on the ground. "Thanks, Queen Esther."

She smiled. "You are welcome, Meshac of the fiery furnace." She leaned over the seat and looked at me. "Next time you might want to take the bus."

We laughed together, and I trudged the last three blocks to the motel. Boy, did that look good.

I picked up my key at the front desk. Loretta was there dusting.

"Where you been?"

"I had some business in Jackson."

"Why'd you leave your key here?"

"I didn't know whether I'd be back tonight or not. Thought you might need it."

She looked at me. "Whatcha got your big bag with you for?"

Yeah, I thought, nosy with a capital N. "You never know what you might need. Now leave me alone. Are you my mama?"

She grinned, and I walked back to my room. All I wanted was my own bed. Thank you, God. I would worry about the sheriff later. If I needed to confess it all and take my medicine like a big girl, then that's what I would do. But for now I needed to keep my head down and my mouth shut.

After a night filled with flying rocks and skulking figures, I opened my eyes and daylight streamed through the blinds. I made it. The next few days I kept to myself, huddled under the covers with Auntie's book. I studied the signs. The silver marks from Aunt Flora's dull pencil underlined the important passages. Made me kind of homesick, too. As I took a load of wash to the laundromat, I spied the phone booth and decided to call home. I dropped in my dimes and quarters and dialed. Auntie answered this time, and I didn't hang up.

"Hello?" Her voice was high and questioning.

"Auntie, this is Meshac."

"Well, I do declare. How're you doing, sweetie?"

I almost melted. "I'm good, Auntie. Just thought I'd check on you all."

I shifted to look out the glass window of the booth. No one was in sight but a yellow tomcat.

"'Bout the same, I reckon." Her voice tasted of home—thick with biscuits and gravy and a cold Dr. Pepper.

"How's Mama?"

"No good at all. Surprised she's still alive."

"Does she know anything?"

"Nope. Just lies in the bed and nibbles at whatever we leave for her."

I heard a car door slam and watched a young woman lug a pillowcase of laundry to the front door.

"Did you get my money at Christmas?"

"Sure did. It came in real handy."

"I'll try and send some more."

"We're making out okay."

"Irene and Roy?"

"They're fine. Irene seems almost happy at times."

We paused as if searching for something else to say.

"You take care of yourself now."

"I will, Aunt Flora. Thanks."

I nearly had the phone hung up when I heard her say my name.

"Yes, ma'am?"

"I saved some things of your mama and daddy's. Thought you might like them."

"Sure." What else could I say?

"Where can I mail them?"

I hesitated. I could picture the sheriff standing at my door shaking a box at me and reading the return address.

"Best to mail it to my friend—Edna Love." I gave her the address. "Thanks, Auntie."

The click of the receiver brought me back to this lonely corner of
Nuanz. I walked over to the laundromat, put the clothes in the dryer,
and watched them tumble along with my thoughts. What a sorry-ass
life I led. Maybe it was time for me to fess up. Maybe that whole deal
in Jackson was karma smacking me in the face. I was right back where I
started from. If I died, I died.

Sure enough, within a week Edna came by the Bluebird Cafe after
the three o'clock coffee break. She dug into that huge purse of hers and
dropped a small, brown-papered package on the counter. "I think this
must be for you."

I tried to act nonchalant, but my heart did a big thump. "Yeah, thanks
for bringing it by."

She waited for me to explain, but I turned and stuck the package
underneath the counter.

When I got home, I wanted to kind of savor the moment. I propped
myself up in bed and stared at Auntie's handwriting—those tall, straight
letters with no slant either way. Her hands had cut this paper, folded it
just so—taped it and wound it with this sturdy piece of saved string.

Inside, wrapped in remnants of the *Wicket Herald* newspaper, lay my
daddy's pocket watch and a pair of my mother's earrings. The earrings
were tiny pearls—too girly for me—but I remembered Mama wearing
them a long time ago. I picked up the pocket watch with the worn
leather strap. Those creases had gone white with age, and the greenish-
black stone still hung from the middle. The watch face was worn, and
the numbers three and five were dim. Daddy wore this every day hooked
through belt loops and stowed in his pocket. He'd wind it on Saturday
night and hold it to my ear so I could hear it tick. I wound it between my
thumb and index fingers, not too tight. I held my breath and with closed
eyes held it to my ear. Nothing. What should I have expected? Maybe
Mr. Flowers could look at it.

I wrapped the watch and earrings back in the newspaper and put
them in the box. Then I crumpled the outside wrapper—just in case.
The box fit in the back corner of my bedside table, nestled against Aunt
Flora's book.

Joe got off the boat the last of February. I was uneasy about seeing him. Then suddenly there he was in the flesh at the Bluebird Cafe. Boy, did he look good. I felt my face flush, and I tried to get busy with the other customers. He stood there and looked at me. Then he walked to the back table and sat down with the men. Thank God Louise was waiting on that table. I skulked back into the kitchen, hoping I could hide until he left.

Every time the kitchen door swung open, I looked out for a glimpse. Finally I had to check on my counter customers. I laid their green tickets beside their plates as I cleared up. As I glanced back, I saw Joe's head above the others. I stared at his back for a few seconds longer than I needed to. He left as I refilled Mr. Snyder's coffee. He stood there staring at me. I looked at him and nodded my head. His face was blank. No emotion at all in his eyes from what I could see with that one glance I gave him. Then he paid and left. My chest hurt. It must have been something I ate.

My eighteenth birthday was February 28. I nearly forgot myself. Last year at this time, I was still at home plotting my revenge on old dead George. Mama didn't even acknowledge my birthday. Irene remembered it the day after. But that didn't matter. I didn't feel like celebrating anything then. I wanted George to leave Irene alone. Funny. One minute you're a mixed-up kid, scared of your own shadow, and the next minute you're a killer. When I raised the gun and took that shot, everything changed. I wondered where I might be on my next birthday. Alone, away from here—warm and loved, or afraid and sad?

For my birthday, I brought home a slice of chess pie and lit a wooden match. "Happy birthday to me." I couldn't even sing it. But I shut my eyes, blew out the flame, and made a wish. God knows I needed all the help I could get.

Gandhi at the Lunch Counter

No one had even come close to solving Noah's murder. The sheriff's investigation was at a standstill. Edna hadn't shared any more letters. I continued to carry my rolled quarters in my pocket, but no one jumped me again. Even Grace had accepted that we were not going to find out who killed Noah. A little boy was dead, and whoever did it could be eating next to us. Time began to dull the senses. Sometimes that's good. Sometimes it pushes things deeper until they come rip-roaring out of nowhere to devour you.

It stayed cold that winter well into March. We grumbled and spent our ordinary days bound up in the still-chilly air and the ensuing chill in our hearts.

It wasn't all that surprising then when Mrs. Florence Howard walked in the front door of the Bluebird Cafe and sat down at the counter. It was a cool March day close to the spring equinox. The forsythia had already bloomed. She brought her six-year-old daughter, who twirled around on a stool until her mama said, "Dorothy, be still now."

Dorothy stopped twisting and folded her little brown hands. Her plaited hair held pink and blue barrettes that said, "Jesus loves me." She looked up at her mama and whispered, "But I can't be still." Miss Florence said nothing but patted her hand.

I came and stood in front of Miss Florence. I didn't look at anybody or anything but her brown eyes and serious face.

"Hidey." It squeaked when it came out of my mouth. I automatically reached into my right pocket for my order pad and felt for the stub of a pencil over my left ear.

"What can I get you today?"

She looked at me, and I felt as if my body soared up out of the tin ceiling past the courthouse bell tower with that one look. No matter what Mr. Adams or the coffee club or the gossipy old women in the cafe said or did, it was just Miss Florence and me right now.

"I'd like a cup of coffee," she said.

"Cream with that?"

She paused again. "Yes. Yes, please."

"And for your little girl?"

"She don't need nothing right now."

I took my time, licked the end of my pencil, and wrote every letter of "coffee with cream" in my best handwriting. "Coming right up."

As I turned toward the coffee urn, I heard the chairs scrape in the back around the men's table. No one said a word. Mr. Rob stood listening behind the swinging door. I could see him through the crack. Big chicken. The men threw down wadded dollar bills and coins and shuffled out. The women, God love them, didn't make a move. Miss Florence sat as still as a statue. Dorothy began to fidget again. I brought the cup and saucer back to Miss Florence, and I admit it was shaking a little bit.

"Thank you," she said. Her voice was low, but it hummed in my ear like soft bass chords on a piano.

"You're welcome," I said back and then I waited. I took a deep breath and thought, "That wasn't so hard." Then I heard more commotion at the ladies' table. They got up in one mass like a flock of old hens, dipping and swaying, picking up their pocketbooks, sweaters hung on the chair backs, and their belongings. Then they marched to the counter and, God bless them again, parked their white asses on every stool they could find. Miss Lewis sat down first next to Miss Florence and Audrey sat beside little Dorothy. Audrey bent over and said to Miss Florence, "How old is your little girl?"

"She was six in August."

"Really, what day?"

"The nineteenth."

"That's my youngest boy's birthday. Does she have trouble with hay fever in the fall?"

"Yes, she does. That ragweed tears her nose up."

"Same with my son, too."

The others quickly took their seats and shifted their purses off their shoulders and onto their laps. They smoothed their skirts, adjusted their glasses, twittered a bit more, and then settled. They finally looked at me and waited.

"Well, what'll it be, ladies?"

I felt like a roulette dealer preparing to take bets. Miss Lewis spoke up first. "I think I'll have another cheese omelet."

"Yeah, that sounds good to me, too."

"Make that another one, Meshac."

"I'll have another order of biscuits and gravy," said Mary Turner, the Methodist preacher's wife.

I took all their orders, made more coffee, and laid the tickets in the window for Rob. He gave me one hard look and shook his head.

"Dadburn women. You don't ever know what they're gonna do," he complained as he started frying bacon and cracking eggs.

"What's that?" I asked.

"Never mind."

The orders were nearly all in when the sheriff arrived with the no-count men to see a counter full of women eating, drinking, and talking about their kids, what they were cooking for supper, and how sorry their husbands were. There just happened to be two brown faces in the middle.

I was amazed at how simple it was, yet how daunting. It took a lot of guts for Miss Florence to even walk into that cafe through the front door. It took a lot of guts for Audrey and Miss Lewis to sit down next to them. Dignity, courage, and coolness ruled. There was no need for a .45 Colt because there was nobody to shoot. Only old ghosts hanging around and getting in our way. If we had known it was going to be that easy, maybe it wouldn't have scared us so.

After the brief sit-in at the Bluebird Cafe, the black people in town mainly went back to eating at their own places. About once a week, one or two blacks would come in dressed in their Sunday best clothes and sit down at the counter for a glass of tea or a cup of coffee. They had never ordered food yet. I was always the one working and usually Edna was somewhere in the cafe. Queen Esther never came in, but I would frequently catch sight of her car sitting across the street.

Maybe it was progress of some sort—I don't know. But what overwhelmed me was the way it was handled. Suddenly people were questioning things. This nonviolent protest idea was something I had never heard of. Stopping violence with nonviolence was completely new, especially in my neighborhood. What makes a movement begin? What stirs us to say the word, to commit the action, to walk through the door, to say "no more"? Is it all our doing or is it forced on us from something bigger than us? Like the seed that suddenly begins to sprout, like the never-ending rotation of the earth, like knowing that tomorrow there would be more light. . . . Maybe goodness would win? Or maybe we should accept whatever the universe gave us.

PART V
FULL CIRCLE
SPRING 1961

Putting the Pieces Together

Anniversaries make me stand still and look back. The earth had followed its yearlong path around the sun, holding steady at the 23-degree tilt. The spring equinox had passed. Suddenly it was a beautiful April night. The moon taunted me. I eased open my door and slipped outside to my favorite chair. I hadn't sat outside since last fall. I didn't want to see Joe, and I was uneasy about the mysterious guy spying on me. I settled in and something tugged my hair from behind—Gracie, of course.

"Hey, squirt, where you been?"

"Nowhere—whatcha doing?"

"Sitting."

She stood there, twisting her hands behind her.

"So wanna sit for a while?"

She propped one knee on the arm of the chair next to me and began peeling the dried paint in long, curling strips from the back of the chair.

"Where's your boyfriend?"

"What boyfriend?" I feigned innocence.

"You know—what's his name."

"He's not my boyfriend." I sounded like the ten-year-old.

Our silence was broken by the sound of footsteps.

"Here he comes now," she whispered. She was so proud of herself, like she had caused this. I looked over my shoulder. Joe was headed straight for us. I wanted to run inside, but I knew I couldn't. He stopped and glared. Was this Glare Day or what?

"Hello, Meshac," he said, stone cold.

"Hello." I couldn't say his name. Grace stood up and put both hands on her hips.

"I'm Grace."

"Yeah, I know that."

He reached down to pick up a stick and began snapping it into small pieces. I looked at him then.

"We need to talk."

I didn't say anything.

"Meshac, did you hear me?"

"I know. Yeah. Okay. Uh, later."

"When later?" He tossed the sticks behind him one at a time.

"Soon, I promise." I wanted him to go away.

He turned and stomped back to his room.

"Why didn't you want to talk to him?"

"Leave well enough alone, Gracie."

Then she disappeared. I can really clear a room with my charm. That shot the rest of my night.

The next morning Joe was waiting for me as I left for work.

"Can I walk you to work?"

"I guess. It's a free world. So they say."

He fell in beside me, and neither of us said a word. Finally he stopped and turned me around in the middle of College Street.

"Look, I know there's something going on I don't know about, but I like you. I think you like me, don't you?"

All I could do was nod my head.

"Well, can't we hang out together?"

How I could say no to that? I took a deep breath. "I don't know. It might get complicated."

"It doesn't have to get complicated. Just hang out. No big deal."

"No big deal?" I'm caving. I can feel it. "Maybe."

We walked to the corner. "Okay . . . but . . . no big deal."

"Sure. That's what I said."

"Just good friends."

"Whatever you say." He threw his hands up in surrender.

I looked at him then with my best stay-clear-of-me look. Of course he grinned.

"Thanks, friend"—sarcastic enough to make me smile a little.

Then he leaned in a bit. "Friends kiss, too, don't they?"

I laughed and punched him in the arm. "Don't push your luck, bud." But it did seem okay then.

So we started hanging out, as we called it. Joe would walk me home from work most nights. We would spend my day off at the park or watching the local baseball games. He hadn't gotten me into the car again, and I was glad of that. Some days I would still say mean things to him, but he ignored it. If he wasn't around, I missed him. He made me feel normal. Me—like safe.

The first of May, Joe left for six weeks of river boating. I was itching to bring things to a close in my life. I had come full circle. Full circle indicated a return to where you began. George. If that slimy SOB had left me alone, none of this would have happened. I wouldn't be in Nuanz, Tennessee, hiding from the law. But I also wouldn't be serving coffee to black folks. I wouldn't even know Grace Robinson or Edna Love or Loretta or Queen.

But does full circle mean it's over? There was unfinished business, not only in Wicket, but also in Nuanz. Anticipation hovered over us like an impending storm. Would it be a loud boom or a slow, steady downpour?

Edna showed me a flood of more threatening letters. They were more vicious since the coffee sipping at the cafe started. I could not figure out who hated me so much, but I thought I knew why. We get what we deserve, but I was ready to try and make amends some way. It was time.

I felt conspicuous in my Bluebird waitress uniform as I took the shortcut across the parking lot of the U-Totem grocery store. Darkness was falling. Edna's house was dimly lit, which probably meant I was the only expected guest. As I got to the back porch, the inside door swung open. Edna waved her hand. "Come on in, hon."

She had on a red silk brocade dressing gown with house slippers encrusted with red stones and gold appliqués. Her fat feet oozed out of the shoes, and the heels were crushed down. The antenna-like chopsticks stuck up in the profile of her backlit French knot. She looked like a queen bee, and I was a drone entering the hive.

We settled down in the den, and after the small talk I said, "Okay, why did you ask me here?"

"Well, I need your help in a little matter."

"What little matter?"

Edna fanned herself with a folded paper and I got a whiff of Fleurs de Rocaille. She then handed it to me. It was another letter.

I unfolded it slowly. "Git rid of Misha or I will. Maybe she needs a swim to. Black and white don't mix."

"Who wrote this?"

"I think I know."

"Do you think he had something to do with Noah?"

The room darkened then; I couldn't see Edna's face clearly.

"I think he either knows or he's the one who did it."

"So why bring me into it?"

Edna shrugged her beautiful shoulders as she leaned over and turned on the lamp. "He knows we're friends, and you do run your mouth a lot."

I sat there for a moment. I was afraid to ask. "Why don't you go to the police?"

"I had my reasons when it first started."

I should have left back in the winter when I was thinking about it.

Dammit, I should have gotten on that bus and left. Now what was I getting into?

I shook my head. "I don't guess there's any way I could just leave, is there?"

"You're grown. I guess it's up to you." Edna crossed her legs, and the shiny shoe bounced up and down.

I thought about George, my mama, Hale's Swamp.

"Edna, there's something I need to say."

I took an extra deep breath, opened my mouth, and for the first time spoke aloud about what happened. It tumbled out of me like a rush of water, and I couldn't have stopped it if I wanted to.

"When I was ten years old, my mother's boyfriend, George, raped me in the back seat of our car." I kept my head down, but the words poured out.

"He took me out of my bed and raped me while my mama was passed out in the house. Nobody knew. I was afraid he would kill us all if I told anybody." My mouth was dry; I tried to lick my lips.

"It went on for two years and then he quit. I never knew why, but later I found my daddy's gun and taught myself how to shoot."

I didn't dare look at Edna. I didn't want to stop talking. The words kept pouring out of me like Morton's salt.

"So I waited and waited for five years. And when he went after my little sister, I lured him out to the gullies and I killed him. That was last March."

I stopped then to catch my breath. A breeze pushed against the windows, and the house sighed. I kept my eyes on those ruby stones on Edna's shoes. She didn't say a word. My uniform stuck to my back, wet with perspiration, but I felt cold.

"This old man, Mr. Hunter, helped me bury him in Hale's Swamp, and I got on the bus and came here. I don't know if somebody's going to come get me or not, but I did what I had to do. If you don't want me around anymore, I understand. Maybe I just need to leave Nuanz anyway."

I got the nerve then to raise my head and look at Edna. She stared back at me. She didn't ask one question. Then I cried like a big ole baby and threw my head into Edna's lap. I cried so my eyes swelled and my insides hurt. I could feel the red silk getting soggy. Finally, when I couldn't cry anymore, Edna stopped patting my shoulder and murmuring. I pushed myself up to sit. The house was quiet and dark with this one circle of light around us.

"Let me get you a drink, and I don't mean a Coca-Cola." Edna came back with two glasses of brandy.

"Take a good swig of this."

It burned all the way down, but it felt good and warm when it hit my stomach. I was wrung out, but strangely relieved.

Edna set her glass on the table beside her. "Well, well, well." She shook her head and smiled at me. Then that chuckle of hers started until she slapped her leg and bent over with her deep, infectious laugh floating out of all that redness. The chopsticks shook back and forth, and as Edna tried to get her breath, I realized I was grinning, too. We both looked at each other and slowly lifted our drinks. "Here's to old dead George, may you never rest in peace, you son of a bitch."

We clinked our glasses together and threw back another big gulp. It didn't burn as bad this time.

"Well . . . I already knew I was a sinner royale, but I had no idea about you, hon."

I sat there numb. I had run my mouth enough for one night.

Edna swirled the brandy in her glass before taking another sip. She pushed herself up out of the cushions and waddled to her bedroom. She brought back a crumpled paper sack and dumped a child's muddy shoe and a torn T-shirt onto the table in front of me.

"Where did you get that?"

"Catfish Somers brought it to me. He found it last fall when he was fishing in the Little Sandy Creek. It washed up on the bank, and he forgot he'd thrown it in his tackle box."

"So is it Noah's?"

"Remember Grace said they left their wet clothes behind the bushes? Noah's were gone when she looked for hers. That's how she figured he had beaten her back to the pool again. But nobody ever found them. He was in his jean shorts when they pulled him from the water. And his tennis shoes were never found."

"So how do you know it's his?"

She reached inside the shoe and pulled out a rabbit's foot.

"I want you to ask Grace if she's ever seen this."

I fidgeted. The rabbit's foot swung on its little gold chain.

"I don't know. I don't know if a little girl ought to be involved in this."

"Why not?" Edna asked. "She's already snooping and spying all over the place, isn't she?"

"Well, that's right." My eyes burned from all my squalling.

"If it turns out to be Noah's or like something Noah had, then we use this to set a trap."

"For who?"

She gave me one of those looks. "For the man who did this."

I shivered again like a ghost had walked over my granny's grave. My voice came out in a whisper. "How do we know we got the right man?"

"Hon, I got eyes and ears everywhere. Trust me."

I sat there a minute, letting the brandy do its magic.

"Give me some time to think about this."

"Sure, hon. But don't take too long."

2

A Dose of Fear

As I started home, I didn't know if it was the brandy making me brave or my come-to-Jesus confession. Let's see, we'd accuse somebody of murdering a little Negro boy in the public swimming pool by waving a muddy T-shirt around with a rabbit's foot. That sounded very reasonable. And who was going to help? Edna Love—the town madam. Payback is hell.

My mind was on Edna's plan to rout out the murderer. I kept going over all the men who came into the cafe and the Oasis. Those whose names I knew and those who were just there in the background. As I crossed College Street and drew near the last stretch of tree-covered walkway, a chill ran up my back. It felt like someone was behind me.

I didn't turn around or slow down. But I could feel something out there. Shake it off, Mesha. Come on, girl. You're nearly home.

I could see the lights in the motel parking lot. I was almost home. Then I felt him run up behind me and push me to the ground. He shoved my head against the sidewalk and fell on top of me. I tried to twist my head around so I could scream, and I felt his hands around my throat. He was heavy. I couldn't breathe. George? I thought I killed you once.

Then as he held me down, I felt a sharp pain against my ribs. There was a noise behind us, and as he looked up, I twisted around and tried to get up. A black shadow jumped from the tree onto his back. It was clawing and kicking, and as the man held me down with his foot, he reached over his back with his arm and swung that screaming buzz saw down hard against the asphalt. It bounced once and crumpled. There was no movement or sound. The man pushed me back down with his foot. I pushed up with all my strength and started crawling toward the body. I screamed, and then he hit me hard across my face. When I came to, there was something wedged in my mouth. I felt sick. Everything hurt, even my toes. Then my heart jumped—Gracie.

As I came to again, I could feel vibration underneath me. I was in a truck, I thought. My head knocked against the gearshift in the floorboard. I was folded over like a sack of flour, and my legs cramped. Something wet ran down my side. My head was covered. When I tried to breathe, the air was warm and smelled like cigarettes. I shook my head from side to side and tried again to breathe. It was hard to get enough air inside me. Don't cry, Mesha. Don't cry. Something ran into my eyes and burned as I squeezed them shut. I couldn't even swallow. Oh, God. There was loud music blaring from the radio. It rang in my head as I tried to think. Where was Gracie?

The truck stopped, and the door squeaked open and shut. The music was gone, and it was quiet. I waited there in a tight ball of fear. He opened the door, leaned over, and said: "Git up now real slow."

I tried again to get a deeper breath, and then I felt a cool dampness on my legs and my feet touched the ground. I couldn't get my bearings and leaned over like an old woman and shuffled forward. My hands were tied behind me. My shoulder ached and the back of my skull felt prickly.

He pushed me forward. I stumbled and fell, hitting my chin. The ground smelled like mud. Was I out in a field? I had no idea how far from town or anybody I was. Would it help if I yelled or make it worse? What was he going to do to me? I wasn't a little girl anymore, was I? He turned me over on my back, and I felt his boot on my chest as if he was standing on top of me. He kicked me in the ribs then.

He grabbed the front of my uniform and pulled me to standing, and I felt something sharp like a knife against my side. Suddenly my feet slid out from under me and I fell again. I rolled over down a bank. I must have blacked out, for when I came to, he had me propped against a tree. My shoulders were pinned back, and I could feel the bark of the tree against my tied hands. I tried to not pass out. He cinched the rope across my chest even tighter as he took the pillowcase off and quickly blindfolded me. I tried to see where I was. It was pitch black and cold. He pulled my hair until the back of my head bore against the trunk. I could smell him like rancid meat poisoned with hate. Then he hit me again and again. I didn't think I could stand it. But I thought, I'm a lot harder to kill than a little kid, you bastard. Do not cry, Mesha. Do not cry.

It didn't feel like there were any tears inside of me anyway. I could hear him gasping for breath. Then I smelled a cigarette. I wiggled a bit, trying to make my shoulders stop screaming at the pain. I could smell my fear—metallic, oily, with a shiver of dread. It reminded me of Daddy's pocketknife after he sharpened it. I licked my lips and tasted salt. He grumbled something. Then I heard him walk away, and the creak of the truck door, or was it the tailgate? I tilted my head back to try and look underneath the blindfold. My hair hurt and my side burned when I tried to take a deep breath. I figured I would be dead in a few minutes.

Then I heard the door slam and the truck start. My heart thudded against my ribs. Was he leaving me here? Don't move. Stay still. Anything is better than being with him. I didn't move and waited. The truck sat there idling, and then he drove away. I was still alive for now.

There was a ball of pain at the base of my head. I felt the bark of the tree trunk all the way down my spine. My legs were numb, and my hands tingled. If I could just form enough spit in my mouth to swallow. I listened with all my might for another human being—that sense of a life near me. I could not form her name, but I thought it as if I was shouting it. Gracie, Gracie, are you there? I heard nothing but my wheezy breath and my heart thumping in my ears. She wasn't here. Had he gone back for her?

After I realized I was alone, I tried to gather some strength. Think, breathe, feel. Then I heard it—water rushing over stones. That waterfall at the creek where Gracie and I went. The quietness receded, and the night sounds began. Listen for something, Meshac—tree frogs or the katydids. See, there they are. If they aren't scared, neither should you be.

The blackness surrounded me like too much cover on a summer night. Something brushed my face, and tiny feet ran down my chest and paused lightly on my hip. I had to move a little. Legs, move. Move, dammit. There, I thought, they obeyed. I turned my head and there seemed to be some give to the rope. I moved my lips and wiggled my jaw. Blind man's bluff. Remember playing that game at home? Arms spread out wide, staggering around the yard. Mama's drying rag tied around my head. I couldn't see a thing. Irene and Roy giggled and then ran screaming everywhere while I shuffled around with outstretched arms. Blind man's bluff. Take a breath in. Come on. Move your shoulder. Yeah, the tree scraped my back but I didn't care. Dig in your heels and bend your legs. Who cares if it hurts? Move—rock back and forth. You ain't dead yet.

Then blackness again. How long was I out? Keep working. Do you want to die out here alone? The frogs stopped their music and everything was dead quiet again. Was someone there?

There was a memory floating somewhere in the dimness. I couldn't open my eyes. Did I even want to try? Then it was almost there. Where was I? There it was again—a drop of something rolled down my face, and a curtain of water surrounded me. I had to . . . but I couldn't. Where was that thought? There, I nearly had it, and then it was gone. Just be still and breathe. Smell the dirt or give up. It's your choice, Mesha. This dirt from which you rose up and were formed. It felt as if someone brushed my hair back from my forehead. Then I heard my daddy laughing and someone was running toward him; was it me? Suddenly, the moon was shining on my quilt, and I could see someone next to me sleeping. Now the ringing in my ears cleared a bit. I heard a bird. It whistled low but insistent. Right now, Meshac, feel your hand. Wiggle your fingers. What do you feel? Is it mud? Will it hold you? Push up. Get your feet underneath you.

I licked my lips and took another breath. My side ached when I took a deep breath, but if I was hurting then it must mean I was still alive. I shifted my shoulder and slid it slightly against the trunk and leaned against my hand. Pushing with my feet, I sat up a little taller against the tree. The rope was too tight to do much more. I waited. I would not die. Not here alone. I would not.

A Dose of Courage

I heard voices. Quiet and low—at least two of them. I tugged again against the tree and tried to make some noise. If it was him, I didn't care. I could not stay here any longer. Then someone said from behind me, "Oh my Lord." I tried to nod my head so they would know I was not dead—not yet. The light was so bright as the blindfold came off, and I saw two brown faces looking at me. I tried to say my name and then nothing.

"Hon, open your eyes. It's time to wake up. Come on now."

The words floated around me. I tried to do what they said—open my eyes—but I couldn't. The light hurt. Please just go away. Then the words came again, and now a pressure on my shoulder. Don't do that, I wanted to say. That hurts. But the words kept coming. "Hon, come on now. Open your eyes. I know you can." It was Edna. What was she doing here? Then I saw her face close to mine, her eyes big and her mouth moving.

"See, there she is. She opened her eyes."

Then it went black again. Tried to open them but no . . . later maybe.

Suddenly my body jerked, and I was awake in a strange room with a throat as dry as dust. My eyes felt glued together. My ears made a rushing sound as I turned my head to see where I was.

"Where am I?"

Edna leaned in and smiled. "You're in the hospital safe and sound."

"Am I alive?"

She laughed. "Well, if you're not, then this is a hell of a place for the afterlife."

I tried to smile, but everything hurt.

The nurse came in to check on me. The stethoscope was cold against my chest. She studied me as she looked into my eyes and held my hand as she felt my pulse. Her hands were soft and warm.

"You gave us a little scare. Dr. Davis will be here in a little bit."

I didn't say a word.

"Lie back and I'll get you some ice water." She nodded at Edna and then closed the door. The spinning had stopped, and I tried to connect what had happened. It was too hard.

"Just tell me."

Edna patted my arm. "Well, hon. Pookie and Big Red found you tied up against a tree down by the Little Sandy Creek. You were in pretty bad shape."

All I could do was nod.

"They picked you up and brought you into town. Pookie carried you a mile or more—ran the whole way. We were all looking for you, of course."

She sat on the edge of the bed, and the movement made me moan as the pain shot through my side.

"Shit. I'm sorry, hon. I forgot."

"What happened?" was all I could say.

"Do you remember anything at all?"

I tried to concentrate. "Walking home from your house and seeing the motel—then it . . ."

She nodded as she patted my hand.

"Then—oh my God. Gracie. Is she?"

Edna stood there. Nothing came out of her mouth. My heart jackhammered against my chest. I tried to sit up but couldn't.

"Is she all right?"

Edna spoke so softly I had to squint to read her lips.

"There was a lot of blood."

Silence as she stared at the door, her arms crossed over her body.

"She hit her head on the asphalt. She's still out like a light."

My voice was hoarse. Edna had to lean closer.

"She jumped out of the tree on top of him. She tried to stop him." I could feel the tears drip off my jaw.

"Hon, she's awful little. You know."

I didn't want to hear any more. I looked away, but I made one thing clear. "Don't you dare let her die."

They wouldn't let me see her, of course. Not for a couple of days. I didn't know for sure if they were lying or not. But on the third day, I swung my legs over the side of the bed and grabbed hold of the bed rail. It hurt like hell, but I had to see if Gracie was okay. I made it to the door before I blacked out. That, of course, made my side start bleeding again, but I demanded that they let me see her. They did. She was peaked and had a big turban of gauze wrapped around her head. But she was breathing, and when I said her name, her eyes flew open.

"So, squirt, where'd you get that big head of yours?"

She didn't say anything—just stared at me. Finally her lips moved. I could barely hear her. "You look like a hant."

"Takes one to know one." That brought a little smile to her face. I couldn't help myself; I touched the side of her face. "Hey, you are a brave little snoop of a girl."

She nodded her head and closed her eyes. "I know."

I turned then and toddled back to my room. I felt steadier on my feet now. Gratitude crawled into bed with me and we slept.

After a few more days, Dr. Davis finally agreed to let me go home.

The sheriff came by to make his official visit. He had been here before, but Edna and I kept evading his questions. This morning it was me and him. I knew it was the official interview when he leaned forward, looking over his glasses at me as solemn as Job.

"Meshac, we've been trying to figure this all out, but I got a few more questions."

I looked at the ceiling and tried to look pitiful. It didn't work.

"I've got the sequence of things. I know you said you felt like somebody was following you." I nodded. "I know you said he put you in a truck . . ." He waited for me to nod again. "He covered your head with something."

"A sack or a pillowcase, I think. He tried to do that before in front of the motel that other time."

The sheriff nodded his head and waited. I heard a door close nearby and someone passed by my room.

"When Pookie found you, you were blindfolded."

I shifted in the bed and tried to reach my water. He stood up and handed me the glass.

"Can you remember anything he said to you or what his voice sounded like?"

I sipped the water before I answered.

"He was a white man. I know that. He smoked a lot. His breathing was hard. I could smell the smoke and his sweat. He stunk. And he was strong, I guess. I saw him throw Gracie way up in the air."

The sheriff nodded now. "Why do you think he left you out there? Did he think you were dead?"

"I don't know, Sheriff. I passed out several times when he kept hitting me. But I was awake when I heard him walk over to the truck. I thought he might have Gracie or her body there, but then he left."

Sheriff Hensley leaned back in the chair. "He might have been coming back to get Gracie and get rid of both of you at the same time."

I had thought of that but I didn't say so. "Do you think he's still here in Nuanz?"

The sheriff stared at me and then shrugged his shoulders. "Who knows? You'd think he'd head out of town, but he could be lying low until . . ." His voice trailed off.

"What, he can try it again?"

"Well, by now he must know we don't know exactly who he is." He waited then as if I could tell him more. I didn't know if it was time to fess up about the letters or not. Edna and I had not discussed our plan again. So as usual, I played dumb. Not a hard thing to do. The sheriff left with the promise to keep an eye on me. "Don't worry. We'll take care of you and Grace. We'll catch him, I promise."

Once I was released from the hospital, Edna wanted me to come home with her. I had had enough of people for a while. I wanted to be alone and told her as much. It still hurt to stand for long, but I could handle this. Loretta brought me a plate from the Bluebird Cafe three days running, and I began to feel nearly normal. But I still left the light on at night.

On the tenth of June, I walked down to the cafe and ate my noon meal there. My customers were glad to see me. Even Rob Adams patted me on my back before he said, "I reckon if you can come eat, you can come to work."

"I can start back tomorrow."

Lawyer Malone stepped up as the spokesman for the men the next morning as I poured their coffee. He cleared his throat. "Meshac, we all took up a collection for you—except for certain skinflints we won't mention."

The men laughed and shifted in their seats, but kept their eyes on me. "We knew Rob wouldn't take care of everything, so we've paid off your hospital bill."

I was floored. "But you shouldn't have done that."

"We don't want to hear any more about it. Just glad you're back here with us." Things got awful quiet. "If you need any of us any time, call, and we'll be right there."

I headed back to the coffee urn. Soon the baseball talk started again and normal descended on us.

I was not ready to be out past dark yet. Grace was still under house arrest (so she said), so I didn't have any visitors. But my loaded gun was in the nightstand, and I told Loretta to not stick her nose where it didn't belong. She grinned. Joe was due home on the twentieth of June.

I settled into my routine, but it wasn't the same, of course. I was always looking over my shoulder and always listening for that hint of someone who could be him. The man. I had trouble sleeping all night, and reading was too hard. I would turn a page and have no idea what I had read. There was anger boiling underneath it all. I knew that. When I did sleep, it was full of dreams—old men in John Deere caps fishing out shoes that turned into grinning skulls, me driving in the dark without any headlights and trying to keep my eyes open, and red spider lilies everywhere. My nights were long, and I kept looking at the clock, waiting for daylight.

It felt like there was something hanging over all of us here in Nuanz. The bruises were fading, but not my anger. Someone was always there at the end of my shift to give me a ride home. I knew they had planned that until Joe got back at least.

I looked for him all day on the twentieth. Mr. Gordon let me out at the motel office, and as I came around the corner, Joe stepped in front of me. I jumped and then stood there staring. Suddenly, I shoved him hard against the wall. All I could see were streaks of light, and I couldn't take a deep enough breath. I was so angry, white-hot trembling angry. He put his hands out to try and hold me, but I slapped them away. Then I grabbed his shirt in a tight ball and butted my head against his stomach.

"Where were you? I needed you."

He mumbled something, and I let go of his shirt and stared up at him.

"What?" I screamed. I pushed him away with both hands hard against his chest.

"Edna—she told me. I didn't know, Mish. I didn't know."

I wanted to hurt him. I swung my purse square against his jaw. Grabbing my puny plastic headband off my head, I threw it hard right at his blue eyes. Then I tore off my shoe and threw that at him hard as I could. I wanted to fight. I wanted him to shove me back, so I could show him that I could hurt him, too. I could. Then I was back in his face screaming, pounding his chest with my fists. He took a step back, and I could feel myself falling. He caught me, and we fell on the ground hard. His arms circled around me, and I felt his heart thumping against my cheek. The heat suffocated me. His hands cupped my head. We sat there together crying until I pulled away and wiped my face on my sleeve like a kid. I looked away.

"Just leave me the hell alone." I looked at him then and repeated very calmly, "Leave me alone."

He handed me my shoe as we stood up, and I limped off toward my room. I was wrung out limp as a dishrag. I lay across the bed, too tired to get undressed. I closed my eyes, and all I could see was his face all screwed up and his mouth moving. "I didn't know."

There was something gnawing at me the next few days that wouldn't let go. My body was healing but not my soul. I filled my day with routine and tried not to think. Finally, the day before the summer solstice, Edna sat down at the counter and looked at me. I wiped the counter all around her and then said, "I'm ready." She hung her purse over her shoulder and said she would pick me up after work.

When I got in the front seat, she handed me the U-Totem grocery sack. I didn't have to look inside. I knew what was there. We pulled up to Rem's and wandered up to the front porch. There were a few folks there. It was still early. The lilac bush beside the steps was opening its purple flowers, and as we pushed ourselves up the steps, I got a whiff of something good cooking. The butterflies in my stomach jumped up to my throat. Edna opened the screen door. I followed and looked around at the customers as they checked out two white ladies coming in the front door of Rem's. My eyes locked with Miss Florence's. Thank God she was standing in the kitchen doorway. I heard the grease popping in the skillet behind her. Rem was behind the bar drying the glasses and stacking them neatly.

"Howdy, ladies," he nodded. "Miss Edna."

"Hello, Rem. How's it going?"

I didn't say a word, but I saw Miss Florence wipe her hands on her apron after she covered the skillet with a lid. She came and stood beside Rem. They were brother and sister. You could see the similarities in their faces—high cheekbones, skin the color of heavy creamed coffee, and bright, steady stares.

"How you doing, Meshac?" said Miss Florence.

"I've been better." I glanced in the mirror behind the bar. My bruises were fading, but my forehead still had that jagged scar over my left eye.

"Would you care for a beer?"

"I thought you'd never ask," I said and fell gratefully onto the first rickety stool my behind could find. Edna pushed against the counter and sat down, too. The sack was between the two of us on the floor. Rem reached into the cooler for two Falstaffs. They were cold and frosted, and he poured each one into a mug without even asking.

"What brings you ladies to our fine establishment tonight?" he asked.

"We're doing a little Woolworthing," I said without cracking a smile. Miss Florence caught my drift, and I could hear her laughing as she moved back to the chicken frying. Rem grinned then.

"Don't y'all be getting something started that I'm gonna have to call the law down here."

"Oh, we'd hate to do that." Edna arched her right eyebrow at him. We leaned forward and sipped our beers in unison. We must have looked like those bobbing plastic ducks at the carnival booth, waiting for someone to choose us. My little finger was still taped up, but I could hold that mug just fine. A couple of the pool players laid some money on the counter for Rem. He nodded and put the folded money in his left shirt pocket. I looked out the window at the lilacs and thought of Grace and Noah lying there spying. The smell of fried chicken drifted from the kitchen. I was ready to get this deal on the road. I poked Edna's foot.

"Rem, we got a little business to take care of, but we need some help from you," said Edna.

"So," he drummed his fingers on the bar.

"Meshac and I have something we want to show you and Miss Florence." Edna reached down and set the sack on top of the bar. It stood there between us, worn and sad. Rem did not look too happy.

"Don't be bringing me a sack full of trouble, Miss Edna."

"I'm not, but this is something that's got to be done." She stood up and reached into the sack and pulled out Noah's muddied T-shirt.

"What am I supposed to know about a little dirty T-shirt?"

"That it belonged to Noah Johnson," Edna said.

"And?"

"It was found in the Little Sandy Creek that runs across Edd Biggs's property."

Rem didn't say anything. Miss Florence stood in the doorway, holding a fork and listening to every word.

Edna continued. "Did Edd Biggs have a run-in here the night of Noah's murder?"

"Who wants to know?" Rem scowled and looked back at his sister.

"We do," I finally croaked. "We want to go to the law with some evidence, and we need some help."

Rem leaned over on his forearms against the bar. Ignoring me, he looked directly at Edna.

"Miss Edna, we don't need to get in all of that."

"Yes, we do, Rem. You know I wouldn't start anything if I didn't think I could handle it."

He shook his head. "This may be more than what you bargained for."

"We want to draw him out and set the trap for him," I said. "We owe it to Noah."

I stood there with my arms folded, a little too brash. I could see my reflection behind Rem—a skinny kid with a big, red scar, squinting in the light. But the real scars didn't show.

Rem stood there a moment. He took the drying rag off his shoulder and picked up another glass. He ran the towel around the outside of the glass, studying it as he spoke.

"How do you think you're gonna do that?"

"Will you tell us what happened that night?" Edna sat back down, and so did I.

"Mr. Biggs is one of my regular backdoor customers. He buys a pint most every night. He pulls up there in the back and somebody comes in with his money." Rem set that glass down and reached for another. "Sometimes I hand him the whiskey, sometimes Albert does. That night Albert waited on him because I was inside closing down. It was Fire Night, and everybody had moved outside. When Albert handed the bottle to Mr. Biggs, it slipped out of Biggs's hand. Albert had already turned around to go back in when he heard the glass breaking. Mr. Biggs started cussing him."

The pool players laughed and someone said, "Rack 'em up again."

"Albert told me what had happened. I went out and told Biggs we were closed. He left then, screeching tires. He's done that before. I didn't think anything about it."

Edna made another circle on the bar with the bottom of her Falstaff bottle. "Did he come back that night?"

"Not that I know of. But like I said, we was real busy. They had shut us down for a few days earlier, and there was a big crowd. When we heard about the drowning, we locked up. There were a few of us left at three thirty when the deputy came by."

I looked over my shoulder. The pool players pretended to concentrate on their game, but I knew they were listening to every word. This was it.

"Okay." Edna gathered up her purse and the sack, and we took one farewell sip of our beers.

"Whatcha gonna do now?"

"We're gonna sit out back in my Caddy until Mr. Biggs pulls up for his pint."

"Oh, hell, ladies, don't be doing that."

"And then Meshac's gonna hop out and take his picture with this camera. And she's gonna say, 'Thank you very much for your picture.' Then if Mr. Biggs happens to see this paper sack, somebody might tell him what's in it."

"And?"

"And maybe refuse to sell him any whiskey," said Miss Florence from the doorway. With a solemn face, she repeated the words: "We reserve the right to refuse service to anyone."

Her brother looked at her and shook his head. He placed the polished glass on the shelf and hung the rag on the corner of the cabinet. I heard the clatter of the balls breaking on the table behind us. He shook his head again and turned around to face us.

"I joined the Navy when I was eighteen. Daddy didn't understand me leaving home like that. Saw the world for a few years and got kind of used to being useful, you know?"

Rem looked out the window for a long moment.

"When I got out, I thought things might be different here. Daddy wanted me to come home. But of course things weren't different here." He rocked back on his heels, and we waited.

"Baby sister always was the spitfire in our family. Damn bossy, too."

Florence smiled, then said again, "We reserve the right to refuse service to anyone."

Rem shook his head and smiled. "And then?"

I spoke up. "And then I jump in Miss Edna's car and hightail it out of here."

"Who's gonna stop him?"

"Nobody, we hope."

Edna and I lowered our voices. Rem leaned in closer and nodded.

It was nearly ten thirty before Mr. Biggs's old black pickup appeared down the alley. Thank God I had just taken a pee break. He eased his truck up behind the back door and blew his horn. He didn't even look around to see if anybody was watching. My hands shook as I picked up the camera from the passenger's side seat with the empty paper bag. I walked in front of the headlights of the truck, real slow. I squinted as I stared into the cab of the pickup at the man. Courage, that was what I needed. Courage.

I walked out of the light to the driver's side. The rumble of the truck filled my head, but I looked at him. "Hidey, Mr. Biggs."

He scowled as he looked at me. His left arm dangled from the window. I brought the camera up to my face, sighted through the viewfinder, closed both eyes, and squeezed. When I opened my eyes, Mr. Biggs had his hand over his face.

"What the hell are you doing?" His voice jarred something inside me.

"Thanks for the picture, Mr. Biggs."

I didn't know where I found the voice to say that, but I did back away from the truck. I waggled the sack at him and tried not to run. About that time, like it was perfectly orchestrated, Rem came to the top step of the porch. I stood there waiting. My legs were shaking, and I held the sack up close to my chest.

"Mr. Biggs," he shouted. Mr. Biggs looked at him, confused.

"What the hell was that about?" he growled, pointing at me.

"She was in here asking questions about a little boy's T-shirt. Said it was found up near your place."

Mr. Biggs mumbled something as he reached into his pocket.

"Here's my two dollars. Give me a pint quick."

Rem walked down the stairs and pulled himself up to his entire military six feet four inches. "We reserve the right to refuse service to anyone."

"What?" It didn't seem to register on Mr. Biggs's face. About that time, three other guys came and stood behind Rem with their pool sticks in hand.

"I said we reserve the right to refuse service to murderers."

Mr. Biggs sat there in a stupor. "You'll regret the day you ever said that, you uppity nigger."

Rem crossed his arms and grinned. "Well, we'll see about that, Mr. Biggs."

That was my signal. I slammed the car door and took off. I spotted the truck in my rearview mirror about the time I made the turn off the square. When I knew he was behind me, I sped up. My heart was racing. My shirt clung to my back. I didn't know how my teeth could chatter when I was sweating like a whore in church. The Caddy's speedometer read forty-five before I knew it. Steady now, girl. You can do this.

I turned off the highway and went about a hundred feet before turning onto Christmasville Road. This was a well-populated road about three miles from city hall. By this time of night, most of the houses were dark. The city streetlights ended at the turnoff. Mr. Biggs kept a pretty good distance from me, and I wondered what he was thinking. Was he angry enough not to realize what I was doing? I hoped so. I slowed down as if I was going to turn in a driveway, and he pulled up behind me and flashed his lights. I looked in the mirror and then pulled away quickly. He continued to tailgate.

"You're so damn easy."

As we continued to drive farther into the country, my pulse rate quickened. I tried to calm down. I thought about home, the stars I used to watch at night when I couldn't sleep. Glancing out the windshield, I saw the stars popped out all over the black sky.

"Let's see. There's the Little Dipper and Orion's Belt. Okay. Help out, old Cassiopeia. Gather up ye gods and decide my fate."

I hesitated the car, sped up over the last hill, pulled into Lover's Lane, and doused my lights, knowing he had seen me. I pulled the car down about midway to the turning-around point Edna and I had decided on previously. There was a stand of trees next to the road.

"Oh, God, ole Buddy of mine, remember me?"

Mr. Biggs pulled his truck up to block my car. Just like I expected. I jumped out and stood there next to the open car window.

"Get out of my way," I said with much more fervor than I felt.

"You little white trash bitch. What'd you think you're doing?"

"What do you mean?"

"Gimme that camera."

"Nope, that's mine."

He started toward the car.

"Do you think I'm stupid?" My voice squeaked on "stupid." He looked at me.

"Yeah."

"I can smell you from here." He stared at me, but he didn't move.

"I've got the shirt and one of his shoes. His grandmother's already identified it. We're gonna get the sheriff to start digging on your side of the creek bank."

"You ain't got no proof of nothing." He started creeping toward me.

"There's an eyewitness that needed a picture of you to be sure."

He stopped then. "Eyewitness to what?"

"You standing there in the bushes watching them swim. Those kids knew somebody was there. Then I guess you followed them back to the pool from Rem's, didn't you?"

His voice was cold and hollow. "I'm gonna teach you a lesson you ain't never learnt. If I could have carried you both, both of you would be dead now."

Then I held up the rabbit's foot. "You old fool. Don't you know kids gotta carry a lucky rabbit foot in their shoes? This is the one found in Noah's shoe right where you tried to bury it. How'd a little colored boy's lucky rabbit's foot get in your backyard?"

"Gimme that. It's mine."

I took a step closer to the car.

"We got a deal, Mr. Biggs?"

"What deal?"

"First you gotta tell me why."

He stood there a moment. I heard an owl hoot and its wings fluttered.

"There's already been a murder on this lane, you know." His voice was low, but I could see his face getting red.

"I know. But plenty of people know I'm out here." I held the sack up where he could see it. I had stopped shaking. "Why?"

He spoke slowly. "'Cause they're not supposed to be here—eating, drinking, and breathing the same air as us."

I lost my train of thought seeing the vileness on his face.

"So you killed him," I said as loud as I dared.

"Yes," he shouted back at me. "I'd watched those two kids—that white girl and black boy—sneaking around town. Running loose all hours of the night. Seeing things they ought not to be seeing. Then that night I seen the little white girl heading up the hill to the pool. I eased my truck down behind the Ag building and walked down by the streetlight. I heard them in the pool. That black boy swimming in the water and getting it all dirtied up. That little white girl acting like it was fine. I would have let it be if they hadn't gone and turned up down at Rem's again spying on me, lying together underneath the bushes. Just like Maxey and Trixie lying together in the back seat of that car. Did you hear what happened to them?"

I tried not to move or blink. I wanted him to keep talking, but his voice and those words were making me sick.

"When I saw them two children again standing there all huddled up together, I thought, 'I can't put up with this any longer.' So I waited for them and followed the boy up to the pool. When he got his clothes out from the hiding place, I just grabbed him and shook him as hard as I could. I didn't hit him but once. But he fell back across the concrete and I started kicking him hard. Then I took his shoes off and threw him in the pool."

He looked at me, then slowly grinned. It reminded me of old dead

George. "Yeah, I killed him and then let him have one more swim in the white man's pool."

He took another step toward me. I leaned over and rested my hand on the car door.

"I should have taken care of you down by the creek, too. If that little girl hadn't jumped me, I would have finished what I started. But turns out y'all didn't know for sure it was me anyway."

"You disgusting bastard."

He started for me then, and everything happened at once. He moved pretty fast for an old man, but I reached inside the car and grabbed my gun. Edna rose up from the back seat and started hollering and floundering around to get out of the car. Bad Eye's truck roared up the lane to block Biggs. This signaled Sun Man and Boy Blue hidden in the trees. Others appeared with them. Their eyes were harsh; their fists clenched. I leaned against the front of the car. What would happen now? They grabbed Mr. Biggs hard, and he tried to get away. He was cussing and spitting. Sun Man and Boy Blue held him, and they managed to push him, all of them like one force moving together. He would nearly go down and more hands would reach and pull him upright until he was pinned against Bad Eye's truck.

I elbowed my way in. My gun cleared a space before me, and I followed. Biggs stared at me, and then he blinked when he saw the gun. I held it two-fisted in front of me.

"All right, guys. Settle down," said Edna.

No one looked at her. No one said a word, but we all stopped. I could hear heavy breathing, and suddenly it was cold and dark, and I didn't know what might happen next.

I took the last few steps inside the circle and let the tip of the barrel rest on Biggs's forehead. He closed his eyes and started to speak.

"Shut up." I held the gun steady. There was no quiver in my hand. A calmness rolled down over me like that quicksand back in Hale's Swamp. Maybe this was the only way to make things right.

Just when it seemed it might tip over to justified violence, the lights of the patrol car strobed across the sky. We looked up and saw the reflection of the lights coming from town. I looked at Biggs again with my gun against his head. One last look. Then I lowered the gun and stepped back. I heard a couple of blows and some groans, and the circle tightened again. We waited.

Then the squad car pulled in at the end of the lane, its white beams bouncing off the darkness. We could hear the squawk of the police radio. The sheriff stepped out of the car.

"What's going on here?"

Mr. Biggs could not even speak. The black men did not move. Grace's head poked up from the sheriff's front seat, and she leaped out of the car and streaked toward me.

"You caught him, didn't you?"

Biggs was a little bolder now that there was no gun against his head. "These people are attacking me."

Grace stopped and looked at him. "You're the one. You're the one who killed Noah and hurt Mesha."

She ran straight for him with her skinny little arms flailing. The men grabbed Biggs and held him upright as Grace landed her pitiful blows on his stomach. She hit and kicked him with a thousand tiny little eleven-year-old, skinny girl blows. He recoiled, from pain or shame, I don't know. The men looked at the sheriff and waited.

"What's going on here, Edna?" The sheriff addressed her first.

I hugged Grace next to me.

"We were just getting some things sorted out."

"What things?"

"Noah."

We looked at Sheriff Hensley. Mr. Biggs hung his head.

"I hope you've got this right, Edna."

"We do, hon."

The sheriff looked at us. The headlights lit our faces, brown and white.

"I'll take him from here." The sheriff moved toward the circle of men. They held onto Biggs.

Sun Man spoke up. "We want to go with you."

The sheriff hesitated, then motioned at the men. "Put him in the back of Bad Eye's truck."

The men were as shocked as we were but hustled around and lifted

Biggs into the back of the truck. Three men rode in the back with him standing up looking over the cab as Bad Eye pulled out onto the highway.

We were a parade like had never been seen before in Nuanz—the sheriff's patrol car, Bad Eye's truck, and Edna's Cadillac. Word spread quickly, and everybody at Rem's Place came over to watch. As the sheriff escorted the prisoner into the jail, Biggs said, "I sure was glad to see a white man come down that road."

"Shut up," said Sheriff Hensley. "You've got one little smart white girl that's going to be the end of you."

We handed the sheriff the real evidence bag, and he said he needed a statement from everybody. It was three in the morning by the time we all finished. The sheriff was satisfied that we had a bona fide case. We started walking to our cars and homes. Aunt Virginia was there to pick up Grace, and Rem, Miss Florence, Edna, and I were discussing everything that had happened. Then Albert came and whispered something in Rem's ear.

"Hell, you crazy boy. Naw. We're not gonna do that."

We waited to see if he would tell us what that was about. Then I saw a light in his eye.

"Y'all wanna have a little fun tonight?"

"Of course," we all said.

Rem grinned. "How about a swim-in then?"

Our trail of cars made its way to the swimming pool. They had filled it the week before, and it would be a little nippy, but we didn't care. We circled our cars—Edna's Caddy, Aunt Virginia's old Ford station wagon, Rem's immaculate Chevrolet, and the raggedy remains of everyone else. Grace's head was lowered. I knew she was thinking about the last stolen swim she had taken here.

"Come on," I whispered as I knelt beside her. "This one's for Noah."

We walked up and raised the fence so the skinny ones could roll under. We managed to squeeze the gate wide enough to let the others in, including Edna. The stars were fading fast. It would be light soon. We removed our shoes and parts of our clothes and stood on the pavement staring at the blue water lapping against the sides of the pool.

"I used to be a pretty good swimmer in my day," said Aunt Virginia.

"I could do a swan dive off the board."

"Get out."

"I could."

Then something I never thought I would see happened. Aunt Virginia turned to Sun Man and said, "Last one in is a rotten egg."

He stared at that old, shriveled-up white woman, and then he grinned. They both hit the water at the same time in classic cannonballs. We all jumped, dived, or slipped into the water and then came up to the surface. Our laughter mixed with the splashing, and the water lapped against the blue tiled pool and spilled out onto the brown concrete sides. We were a little embarrassed by this closeness that we were not used to. But it felt like it was going to be okay.

They drained the pool the following day, of course. It took ten days to refill and warm up enough to swim in.

Epilogue

On this bright fall day, Joe and I were going on a date in his car. We hadn't gotten around to deciding what our thing was. I liked being with Joe when he was in town. But I also liked being on my own. Joe couldn't quite figure me out, so he said. Maybe I had too many other demons to take care of first. But we tried to get along and have some fun. He wanted to protect me from any danger, but I couldn't say for sure that I wanted him to protect me. Sometimes it smothered me like too much wind in your face.

Tonight I wanted to look pretty for once, so I decided to wear Mama's earrings. Going to the bedside table drawer, I took Daddy's gun out first and laid it on the bed. There sat the package at the back of the drawer, all wrapped up like Aunt Flora had sent to me. I sat down, and the gun felt good and heavy there beside me.

I unwrapped the newspaper Aunt Flora had wrapped the box in. "The Wicket Herald—All the News That Is the News," the masthead stated in large, black type with the date below—November 21, 1960. I held the pearl earrings in my right hand as I took the first one and screwed it tight on my left ear. I glanced at the hometown news. There was a dim photo of two old men dressed in their overalls in front of the Phillips Feed Store. The headline read: "Bodies Discovered—Hale's Swamp." I skimmed the article. "Oh my God." Grabbing the paper, I stood by the lamp so I could see it clearly and read it aloud to be sure I understood:

"The bodies of two local citizens were found in Hale's Swamp late last week. Local duck hunters were building a blind for the upcoming season, which opens December 1. They discovered the bodies wedged underneath a large cypress tree that had fallen across an inlet used to cross into the deadening area. The teenagers came to town, and the local sheriff accompanied them back to the site. Sheriff Tanner reported that it looked as if the men were setting beaver traps and were struck by the tree. Large amounts of debris in the shallow water indicated the storm from last week may have caused the tree to fall. They left no known survivors. If anyone has any information about Mr. John Hunter, 84, or Mr. Roy Hill, 88, please contact local authorities. Burials for both men were held last week at Oakwood Cemetery."

I had to sit down.

Joe knocked on the door at six sharp, and I was eager to go. He drove through town, and as we crossed the overhead bridge, I asked him to pull over.

Joe's eyes questioned, but he did as I asked. I got out by myself. "Gimme a minute."

I stood on the edge of the bridge. It was quiet except for the sound of the rushing river. The fall rains had made the current swift. I didn't know where this river ended. It might run all the way down to the Gulf of Mexico, mingling with a thousand other rivers and streams. I knew each spring the winter snow melted up north, and the rivers filled up everywhere as they flowed toward the ocean. After a dry summer spell, the rain always returned. The water always kept moving.

The river was muddy and full of branches. Two boulders were worn smooth from seasons of rushing water. There was a turned-over bucket someone had sat on this summer while they fished. The kudzu trailed up a cottonwood tree that stood near the bank with its white trunk shining. I could hear Preacher Doaks's deep, rich voice: "Then He took His hand and scooped out the earth so the river could run through it."

"Now, Meshac." I closed my eyes, trying to picture Daddy again. I leaned against the railing and wished for him one last time. Then I opened my eyes and heaved that bundle as hard as I could over the edge. The sack with Daddy's gun made a tiny splash as it landed. I watched as it sank underneath the overhanging yellow leaves.

Every equinox, the sun sets right smack dab in the middle of Highway 104 leading west out of Nuanz. If you start down the hill at that exact moment, the sun sits there at the end of the road like a holy portal. Its shimmering beauty fills up the sky and yourself if you're paying attention. The very next day, the sun begins either its northern swing up in the spring or its southern swing down in the autumn. No matter what we do or don't do—nothing will ever change that.

We may deny our fellow man food, shelter, dignity, and equality. We may snuff out innocent lives, seek revenge for wrongs, or suffer our beliefs in silence. We may learn from our own experiences or others' examples or not. But there is a force that is let loose by the tilt of the earth and the pull of the planets that determines our fate in part. The rest of it is up to us. I believe that. I really do.

About the Author

Nancy Hall was born and raised in Trenton, Tennessee—home of both illustrious and ordinary folks who taught her a lot about living. She received a bachelor of science degree in education from the University of Tennessee–Martin with a major in English and a minor in Spanish. Her master's degree was in curriculum and instruction.

After more than a decade of high school teaching, Nancy worked for fifteen years in the insurance industry, where she specialized in commercial insurance and agency management. She then worked under the Tennessee Department of Education with the Tennessee Infant Parents Services as a parent advisor with developmentally delayed children. Her working years were intertwined with community theater work, writing, and raising a family. She serves as curator/director of the Fred Culp Historical Museum.

In 1995, Hall discovered yoga, which she says saved her life—twice. She is a registered yoga teacher at the 500-hour level and a Level 2 yoga therapist. She continues to practice and teach in these fields today. She states: "Writing and yoga are a natural link between the physicality of the ordinary world and the inner work required for meditation, exploration, and understanding. Practicing yoga and paying attention are the two vital parts of my writing life."

Hall was chairman of the Gibson County Library Board and helped organize the Nite Lite Theatre. She is a Master Gardener and loyal Tennessee Vols fan. She was the first woman to serve as the foreperson for the Gibson County Grand Jury and has served under two judges. She helped establish the Fred Culp Historical Museum and worked for more than four years in preserving and recording a vast collection of local history gathered by her teacher, Frederick Culp. She and her husband renovated a grain bin known as the Diva Den, where she writes, teaches yoga, and watches sunsets.

Printed in the

CPSIA information can be obtained
at www.ICGtesting.com
Printed in the USA
FSHW021911130120
66046FS